Earthbound With a Gift

Jenny Beet

Published by

EarthBound Books

http://www.facebook.com/mattbradfieldphotographyaustralia

http://www.instagram.com/mattbradfieldphotography

For my family: my best friend and our kids – thanks for putting up with me! I love you guys more than Lister loves curries.

And big thanks to my friends Catherine Franks for believing, and to Sandy Coghlan for always having an answer! How can I ever repay you? If this book leaves you wondering if there is an after-life, grab yourself a copy of Sandy's book "Heaven Knows"

Chapter One

What's that buzzing? Swat it!

Can't

Move

Hand

Bright lights blinding.

Turn it off. Hurts my eyes.

Bleep. Bleep. Bleep.

Stop talking. Let me sleep....

*****

Bleep.

Bleeeeep, bleep.

Machines are all talking in a language of their own, rhythmical and loud, yet strangely reassuring. Somewhere farther away - voices echoed. Footsteps, laughter and an unfamiliar smell filled the air around him: *God that smell — what is it?* He tried to sniff but something foreign obstructed his nose. His throat also felt constricted. He struggled to swallow with a mouth that felt like something had crawled in there and died. Noah had been drunk once before at a friend's party which had quickly got out of hand. Waking up the following morning he had felt like death. This felt a million times worse.

Slowly, cautiously, he opened his eyes. He blinked several times and winced at the incessant pounding in his head. Wanting to move, but afraid he couldn't bear the pain, he stared straight up from his prone position. His eyes focused on an unfamiliar ceiling made from white, polystyrene tiles; the square directly above his bed a fluorescent light flickered lazily behind a frosted plastic covering. He squinted as the light burned into his eyes, blinking several times before they focused enough to take in more of his surroundings.

This was an unfamiliar, large room with stark, white walls. Clean. Clinical. In the left corner, an old, bulky television hung lifelessly half way up the wall from a hinged metal arm. Noah tried lifting his hand to remove the annoying obstruction stuck up his nose. His arm fell, refusing to budge, like it was out of his control. He tried moving his legs, he couldn't.

Hospital? Holy shit! How did I end up in hospital?

Am I paralysed?

He had to move. Closing his eyes, he focused all his strength on his leg and arm.

Move. Move. Move.

Noah's leg kicked as his arm flicked up at the same time — he must have looked comical, like one of those puppets on Thunderbirds. The relief welled up inside so strong it made him want to cry. Why was he in hospital?

His mind flashed back to the beach. Noah had gone there to sketch, and for some peace and quiet. He'd taken Jess with him and was playing fetch with her when she took off up the beach as though she'd spotted something. There wasn't another soul around though...except for the boy on the dragon head rock. The boy! A huge wave had lifted up and taken the small child into the ocean. Panic rose from Noah's gut like burning bile as he saw himself wading out and diving under to reach the limp figure just as it slipped beneath the water for a second time. Had he been able to push the boy onto the rock to safety? And in that instant, hadn't he seen a girl? He could swear he had. She stood further up the beach with Jess and smiled at him as she watched. Noah winced as he recalled the moment after, a blinding flash of pain in the back of his head and then – nothing.

"Is the boy okay?" He whispered his thoughts as he tried to turn his head, but the throbbing made him feel instantly sick, and his vision blurred momentarily.

"Noah? Oh my God — nurse he's come 'round! NURSE!" His mum's familiar, shrill voice detonated inside Noah's head; the pain spread through his body with a flash of immense heat. She shrieked once more for the nurse, and he heard her heels click out of the room.

"Great to have you back, son." The soft sound of his father's voice made Noah turn his head again, this time so slowly to his right. He tried to smile but grimaced at the pain shooting from the back of his head through his eyes.

"That was a brave thing you did, Noah Cooper. Brave, but stupid. If you are planning to enjoy your seventeenth birthday in two months, I suggest you leave the heroics to someone wearing a cape next time." Love and relief punctuated his dad's words. "And yes, the lad's fine, thanks to you."

Noah closed his eyes. He couldn't distinguish if sweat or tears were responsible for his drenched face.

"How are you feeling?" The chair creaked as his dad stood.

"...like I need to re-spawn." Noah grimaced again. It hurt to think, let alone talk.

His dad looked awkward dressed in the only suit he owned. Tom Cooper was more accustomed to wearing greasy overalls. Noah wondered for a moment whether his parents were going to a funeral. Even his dad's curls were strangely forced flat against his head; it must have been a desperate attempt to make him look smarter than he normally did. Noah struggled to fill his lungs with air, his heart began to palpitate. He couldn't bear to be left alone in this place.

His dad leaned forward and gently squeezed Noah's shoulder.

A blinding, blue flash filled the room as though the florescent tube above him had spectacularly exploded; Noah was sure everyone in the building must have been able to see it. The pain bounced around inside his head and then it shot out through his eyes, which had turned the scene of the hospital room into a smoky, grey fog. As the mist cleared, a picture came into focus and Noah could see himself, lying lifeless on the hospital bed, doctors and nurses hovering around him talking incoherently. For one brief second, Noah thought he must be dead. In yet another moment, he saw his mum slumped on a plastic seat in a long, dreary corridor, sobbing uncontrollably — he could hear his dad's voice trying desperately to comfort her while needing comfort, himself. He could see this scene as clear as day, but he could also *feel* it happening.

The scene shifted again, as though someone had changed the channel in his mind with the touch of a button on a remote control. Now he saw a tall, worn-faced man with a smile that didn't quite light up his tired blue eyes. The man talked about Noah – using medical terms he didn't understand. "...brain injury...possible subdural hematoma...monitoring the pressure..." He thought he could sense – no, he *knew* he could feel it, almost taste it, the relief in his dad to see Noah conscious. Everything would be alright.

Noah blinked, and the images disappeared instantaneously. His body jolted in the bed and brought him back to the moment. He stared into the familiar grey, watery eyes of his dad who had released his hand from Noah's shoulder.

What the hell is happening to me? Did I just have an out of body experience? Why did it feel like I saw it all through dad's eyes?

"You gave me and your mum quite a scare, son. You've been out of it for three days." Noah nodded silently. He tried processing the images he had seen.

He heard the familiar staccato of heels hurrying back up the corridor. This time, he managed to produce a grin when his mother walked back into the room with a nurse hot on her heels.

"Hi mum." He studied the sun-weathered face he knew so well; it looked pale in contrast to the dark, puffy circles under her green eyes. She cupped her nose with her hands; something Noah had seen her do on the very few occasions something happened to render her speechless. He couldn't help notice the tremble in those hands, and was sure he could see more grey among the auburn hair framing her face than there had been before.

She walked to the left side of his bed and raised her hands. For one horrible moment Noah flinched, believing she might slap him for all the worry he'd put her through. Instead, she placed them tenderly either side of his cheeks, bent over and kissed him softly on the forehead.

With the first touch of her hands, a searing flash of light filled the room followed by massive waves of emotions and that fog in front of his eyes once again. He blinked, like a camera adjusting its range finder; the mist lifted and Noah watched a scene in the car park at the beach. He observed an

5

ambulance and a surfer, still in his wet suit, explaining to a paramedic what had happened. He saw Jess, pacing up and down next to the ambulance. He could feel his mother's gratitude to this stranger for saving her son's life; he could also feel her pain, and it was more than he could bear. He saw the young boy sitting in the ambulance with a blanket around his tiny shoulders; a paramedic giving comfort as the poor boy sobbed with great huge gulps about his lost fishing rod, and how his dad would kill him when he found out. This entire scene he had experienced in the moment it took for his mum to kiss him.

"How are you feeling, love?" She walked back around the bed and sat down next to his dad, too happy to notice him fiddling with his tie, like someone not used to wearing one.

Scared shitless! Freaking confused! Like I'm losing my mind while climbing into yours and Dad's!!! What the hell is going on?

Noah swallowed the huge lump in his throat and concentrated on not blubbering like a baby in front of them, when it was all he wanted to do. Instead, he knew he had to be brave for their sake's — he couldn't be anything else after seeing what he'd put them through.

"I could murder a cheeseburger!"

Chapter Two

Noah spent the next three days doing nothing in between a whole lot of sleeping. For once, he wished his mum didn't run a business from home. More than anything, he wanted to be alone.

Dina Cooper fussed over him like a mother hen, clucking and tutting whenever he pulled himself up from the couch. Being waited on by his mum wasn't so bad, but he couldn't handle not being able to have his friends visit. She kept insisting he needed the rest. It was driving him mad, but that wasn't the only thing.

Why had he suddenly developed these strange powers of being able to see inside his family's minds from the slightest touch? Was this some bizarre side effect from the whack on the back of the head from a huge chunk of driftwood? Or was it something that would disappear along with the throbbing headache and aching teeth. He hoped to hell that would be the case. He hadn't told his parents. He didn't think they'd believe him anyway, and even more certain Kayla, his big sister, wouldn't. They'd probably all assume he'd acquired some kind of brain injury in the accident and fuss over him even more. He couldn't handle that. Besides, he was still trying to work out whether this gift of his would prove to be a good thing or a really bad one.

The worst experience welcomed him when arriving home from hospital. Kayla hugged him, like she really cared, as soon as he'd climbed out of the car. He had 'seen' what his sister had been up to while he'd been lying in hospital, with his mum and dad hardly leaving his side.

Kayla bunked off school to spend time with her weird boyfriend. Christ that was only the half of it. Delving into Kayla's mind in the moment of that hug gave him enough evidence to get her grounded for the rest of her life, and most definitely more information than any brother should know about his sister. However, despite the way she always treated Noah, he did understand how much she cared for him, too, and he felt touched.

It didn't last long, though. Kayla soon acted annoyed at how everyone was treating him with kid gloves, and she went back to treating him like she didn't care.

"Can I get you something to eat, love?" Mum called from the kitchen, it had been all of five minutes since she'd asked him before.

"I'd like a cheese toasty, Mum." He heard Kayla call out from her room. Nothing was missed in a small house.

"No, I'm fine, just going to my room." Noah paused for a second hoping to stop his head spinning as a wave of nausea washed over him and filled his mouth with saliva. He closed his eyes and wondered if this would ever stop.

He collapsed onto his bed, noticing it had been made. Noah swore under his breath. His mum had even put away all the clothes he'd left lying on the floor, and tidied up the pile of unfinished homework on his desk. The intrusion irritated him and was followed by a serving of guilt as he told himself she did it because she cared. Since the accident, she couldn't do enough for him, and his dad had been almost as bad. It was a blessing his dad spent so much time running his own mechanics workshop; otherwise he'd be fussing over him too.

Why can't they leave him be. At least then there would be

no chance of them hugging him or touching his shoulder with concern. He couldn't bear to see any more of their emotions or thoughts, trying to deal with his own were more than he could handle right now.

Noah reached across to his bedside table and grabbed his iPod. Pushing the buds into his ears, he closed his eyes and lay back on the bed. He almost looked forward to going back to school. As he drifted into the realm of sleep once again, he found himself in the same dream he'd had repeatedly since waking up in hospital.

*****

He stood on the beach with the mystery girl. She was beautiful, her dark-brown hair, wavy, like she had left it in wet braids to dry over-night. It completely covered her back like a thick, silky blanket. Noah lifted his hand — wanting to trace its path to the thin ends touching the top curve of her bottom. Her face was pale and flawless, like a perfectly formed mannequin as she turned to look at him. She smiled a smile that only comes from knowing a person for a lifetime. He mirrored her smile with sadness and regret of not knowing anything about her. Walking towards her, the sand felt cold between his toes, but she seemed to be getting farther and farther away from him. He tried to run; panicking, because his legs would not move. He was sinking and calling out to her as he watched helplessly while she disappeared down the dark tunnel until consciousness pulled him back and he woke with a jolt

Chapter Three

School: all those kids pushing and shoving in the hallway before class, something Noah hadn't even considered. If he had, he might have preferred to stay home a little longer.

That first morning was a killer. He hadn't prepared himself for the surge of thoughts, emotions and images from so many of the students. For some reason, he had assumed his new ability would be isolated to his family. Walking through the double doors into the hallway of the school he felt like a lightening conductor, blue flashes filled every space of his head with every push and shove. It didn't need to be skin on skin. A shoulder bumping into his, an elbow in his back, every fleeting touch was enough to take over his mind. He desperately tried to process all the images swirling around inside his head.

How the hell could there be so many unhappy kids in one school?

It was too much. Information overload, so to speak. His ears filled with a hundred different voices, pictures played out in his mind, but nothing made sense. Everything layered into one confused jumble. Noah wanted to scream to make it all stop. His knees buckled, and for one scary moment, he was sure he would faint.

"Well what do ya know; it's the all conquering hero." Noah steadied himself before spinning around to the familiar voice.

"How're things, Nick?" Noah tried to sound calmer than he felt. He winced as he could see where this was going.

Nick threw his arm around Noah's shoulder and started to dig into his hair, looking for signs of the accident.

That flash again, came instantly with Nick's contact, and then the images, too many images. He saw Nick at home arguing with his dad. Mr. Papadopolous might have only been a short man, but the anger in his small, black eyes made him look like someone ready to throw fists. Noah wondered why Nick had never said anything about that to him before. Perhaps it was because Noah had always seen Nick's dad as being a good bloke. He had said as much to Nick many times. Then he saw images of their biology teacher, Mr. Sylvester, but the feelings were all wrong. Mr. Sylvester was the only approachable teacher in school — still young enough to relate to them all, but old enough to have wisdom he cared to share. This tall, dark haired, great humoured guy Noah knew all the girls were crazy about him – in that moment he realized his friend Nick had a crush on him! What the hell did this mean? Was Nick, one of his best mates since primary school, gay?

Noah shrugged his shoulders knocking off his friend's arm in a moment of sheer panic.

Luckily, Nick hadn't read anything into the action.

"Oh man, not one stitch? I thought you'd at least have stitches!" He sounded disappointed, and Noah laughed at his old friend trying desperately to shake off the images he'd seen.

"Well, you know me, didn't want to ruin the hair!" Noah brushed a shaky hand coolly through his hair mimicking his friend.

"Sorry man, but that already happened a long time ago." Nick touched his own short, spiky, black hair. There wasn't one out of place. Nick would never allow there to be. Two girls from their class walked past and pretended to swoon. It never went unnoticed to Noah that most girls didn't need to pretend around Nick. He was definitely what they'd call a 'chick magnet'. Nick stood taller than Noah – always had – his olive skin and dark eyes made it easy to see past his rather long Greek nose. Somehow he'd managed to grow from this gangly, awkward kid and who had been picked on cruelly in first grade to this overconfident guy who could pull any girl he wanted. Maybe this magnet was attracting all the wrong sorts.

The pair grabbed the books needed from their lockers with little enthusiasm for the day ahead while Nick waffled on endlessly about the accident, and asked what it felt like to die. Noah's thoughts turned once again to the girl on the beach. He had to find out all about her.

Suddenly two soft hands covered his eyes making him jump. In an instant flash, he knew they were Mel's. He saw her standing by his hospital bed, her face wet with tears. He saw her in her room at home, crying and worrying about him.

"Hi Melanie," Noah turned around and smiled at her friendly familiar face.

"Don't call me that. You make me feel like I've done something wrong. Oh, by the way, it's not my fault I didn't come round to see you at home — your mum's turned into some Gestapo leader or something, she wouldn't let me. It's great to see you back though, knucklehead!" She grinned at him. Noah suddenly felt weird to know she cared so much. He loved to see her smile — she'd spent an awful long time with a mouth full of braces to fix her 'Bugs Bunny' teeth, which were now perfectly aligned, and he had watched her learn to smile all over again. Her grin reached her eyes; funny how he'd never noticed they were hazel before; like dark chocolate flecked with pistachio nuts.

Noah had known Mel longer than he'd known Nick. She used to live three houses away and had hung onto the fence, chatting away to him and his family the day they'd moved in.

She'd even helped him unpack the boxes in his new bedroom, and then showed him the cubby house she'd built in the empty block next to her home. He could still remember how upset she was when it came to her family moving four years ago. She couldn't see the point of it. Why go to so much trouble just to move to the next suburb? He'd helped her pack the boxes for her room and reassured her it wouldn't change a thing between them. And naturally, it hadn't.

The buzzer sounded, and they filed into their classroom.

If he thought the teachers would go easy on him after his accident, he was sorely mistaken. Noah cussed when the teacher gave him an extra three days to finish the homework he hadn't done, and given a pile of extra work on top of that. *Great. Just great.*

He did, however, for that first day at least; enjoy the attention he got from his fellow students. It is funny how someone can go through three years of high school hardly being noticed and suddenly become interesting overnight.

Noah counted down the seconds until the last buzzer went. At the end of school, he walked with his two best friends to the old gate at the side entrance, which had been made into a monument of scratched initials; theirs had also taken pride of place since the first week of high school. The three of them said their goodbyes and each went off in different directions. The day had been so full on he'd hardly had a chance to talk about the accident with his friends. He wanted to tell them about the girl he'd seen, except something stopped him, that same something was telling him to go to the beach that afternoon. She'd be there. He knew she would be.

Chapter Four

Noah knew how lucky they were the moment they moved to the peninsula. His folks would keep telling him how Australia was a lucky country, but it got a whole lot better once they'd moved to White Cliffs. You only had to witness the population swell each summer to understand its attraction. Appreciation for its beautiful beaches and spectacular hinterland grew as he did.

Home was a white weatherboard with sea blue windows and door. Like so many of the houses in the area, it had been a holiday home before they moved in; simply painted in neutral colours. And just like the house, the garden had been a blank canvas too. It hadn't taken his folks long to make it home.

Now the place felt so small. His mum always complained there wasn't enough room for any more stuff, but only because she was so terrible at organizing. Things seemed to get piled up in the hope somewhere suitable would be found for them to live. Places never seemed to be found, and the piles multiplied.

Dad claimed the yard as his domain right from the start. He loved his garden. He'd planted and created everything; from the ferns under the bull nose veranda, to the fruit trees and the barbecue out the back.

He'd also filled every other available space down the driveway and backyard with cars, all in various states of repair — the perks of being a mechanic – or the downfall of being a mechanic's wife as his mum would say.

Jess pulled enthusiastically on her lead. She only got decent walks with Noah, and he could tell she'd missed it almost as much as he had. He sneaked out the house quietly, desperate not to get caught by his mum.

The beach was a short, uphill stroll from their home. Noah could hear the ocean beckoning him as he walked down the sandy track. His heart began to pound as he wiped his clammy hands down his jeans.

Jess charged ahead and flew down the steps in a moment. Noah took his time. As his first opportunity to return in what felt like weeks, he didn't want to miss a thing. Noah paused with each step to look up and down the coastline. The beach was deserted; his shoulders dropped with disappointment. Opening his mouth wide, he sucked in the cool air with a deep yawn and winced at the sudden, sharp pain at the back of his mouth. He swore out loud at the thought of an impending visit to the dentist.

It was an intimate little beach. The horseshoe cove was secluded from the more popular surf beaches either side of the sandstone cliffs. A rocky ledge to his right formed a platform that curved back around onto itself creating a ready made pool safe for swimming away from the rip. Jutting out at the edge was the dragon head rock. The tide was well in this time. The dragon's head was hardly visible above the foaming waves. No boy fishing from the top of it today. Seaweed formed a regimental line between the oceans edge and the sandy shore. The pungent smell of it invaded his nose. At the bottom step Noah pulled the tennis ball from his pocket and threw it half-heartedly in Jess's direction. It flew over her head and landed in the sand in front of her, but she had no interest in it today. She took off up the beach towards the sandstone cliff face. Noah groaned as he stooped to pick up the discarded toy. Straightening himself he pushed the sandy ball back into his pocket and looked ahead.

The girl was there! How had he missed her sitting crossed legged on the sand? She was laughing at Jess as the excited dog bounced around her like they were old friends.

Noah tried to swallow but had forgotten how. He walked up to her trying to think of the right thing to say, but his tongue was stuck to the roof of his mouth.

"Sorry about my dog — I think she likes you." It sounded dumb, but it was all he could manage to say. He needed to focus on stopping himself from falling since his legs had turned to jelly.

"That's okay. She's gorgeous, and I love dogs." Her words were silky like her hair. She smiled the smile he'd seen in his dreams as she patted the sand to the left of her.

"Care for a seat? I promise not to bite." Her green eyes twinkled playfully. Noah tried to look casual as he sat on the sand her hand had touched moments before.

"I'm Noah Cooper and this is Jess....haven't I seen you before?" Oh God, had he really said that?

"Noah? That's very appropriate. It's nice to meet you, Noah Cooper. I'm Sarah Nicholson and, yes, I come here often." What the heck did she mean by that? She was still playing with him — Noah felt the heat in his cheeks.

She held out her hand to shake and Noah took it quickly, eager to learn more about her from that brief touch. After shaking for a moment, he reluctantly let go and stared wide eyed at her.

Sarah giggled as though she knew he'd learned absolutely nothing about her.

Why the hell did it have to be this very moment his revealing powers would leave him?

"Do you live around here?" It wasn't much, but it was a start.

"My family has a holiday home here. We've been here every summer since I can remember." In eleven years how could he have not seen her before?

"What about now?" He couldn't hide his curiosity. She looked like a summer tourist in her white dress and leather sandals even though the season had ended a few weeks before.

"Well, let's just say it's an unscheduled business holiday." Sarah appeared coy suddenly, and perhaps unsure about opening up to him.

They sat in silence for a moment while Noah gathered his thoughts, and his courage, to ask what he really needed to know.

"Did you see..? Were you at the beach when..? Did you hear about the boy who was rescued here two weeks ago?" Finally, he'd got it out.

Sarah had been playing with the sand – the thick grains like raw sugar – her eyes were looking down at her hands while he spoke. She glanced up at him as Noah desperately tried to read her thoughts.

"I'd heard about that. Apparently he owes his life to a very brave boy, someone about your age, or so I believe." Her eyes were twinkling again. Why did she have to do that?

Noah could feel himself blushing again and broke eye contact. Jess sat down next to him and pawed his leg — looking for the ball. He pushed her away a little more roughly than he'd meant to.

Why is she making this so difficult? Noah thought as he punched the pile of sand he'd been building next to his leg.

He stood up then, looking at his watch, "I'm sorry, Sarah, but I have to go."

The meeting hadn't gone the way he'd hoped.

"Oh that's a shame, Noah. We've only just started to get to know each other." She didn't look that disappointed. In fact, Noah couldn't work out what her thoughts or feelings were, and this annoyed him even more.

"We'll see each other again." Sarah said.

Noah's head felt like mush, he was completely bewildered by this girl — she'd clearly made a point of saying it like it was a statement and not a question.

"I guess so. See you around, Sarah." He turned away and walked off. As he reached the steps he was panting, his hair dripped down the side of his face and the pulsing pain in the back of his head felt unbearable.

On the slow walk home, he played out the scene in his mind, recalling word for word what she had said to him. But it was the way she'd said, '...we've only just started to get to know each other' that got to him. How weird she could say that when she'd not even asked him one question.

So caught up in his own thoughts, Noah didn't see the wet-suit wearing man carrying a surfboard until he almost ran into him.

"Hey dude, how've you been?" He spoke like he looked — like an aging hippy, but his weather-beaten face was warm and friendly. It took a moment for Noah to realise it was the man he'd seen through his mum's eyes – the surfer in the car park, explaining how he'd pulled Noah unconscious from the waves.

"I'm doing well — you were there on the beach that day...?" He held out his hand genuinely pleased to meet the guy who had saved him.

"Mark Bolton. And no worries, any time dude. I've seen many a strong swimmer get into trouble down there. But that plank of wood was no reward for saving a young kid's life."

The flashes were barely noticeable to Noah now, but this one came as quite a surprise since he thought whatever power he'd gained from the accident had left him down on the beach with Sarah. Obviously not. It was still there.

He saw Mark running down the beach, and himself being knocked under by the huge piecc of driftwood. *Christ, no wonder my head still hurts!* He also saw the boy sobbing on the rock after his ordeal, but he didn't see anyone else on the beach. Why couldn't he see Sarah?

Chapter Five

Noah managed to drag himself to school for the rest of the week, his new super power still well and truly with him. He began to harness the skills to better his advantage, like with the biology test Mr. Sylvester gave them on Thursday. Noah had pushed past him while walking into the classroom and managed to 'see' almost all of the answers. It was lucky because he'd studied all the wrong things the night before.

He'd also found out Laura Penrose, the blonde with huge breasts from two grades above, fancied him. It would only be because of his new found hero status as she'd never given him a second glance before the accident.

Noah had issues with his friends, though. He couldn't help but see Nick differently now he knew about his crush on Mr. Sylvester. It didn't so much bother him he might be gay, he couldn't quite understand it yet, but he didn't have a problem with it either. What did bug him was Nick hadn't been able to confide in him, and they were supposed to be best friends.

Mel was a puzzle. He knew she cared about him a lot — heck, he felt the same about her. They'd been around each other for a long time, and he'd never had a problem telling her everything or vice versa, except now something was holding him back. He wanted to tell her about his new powers, but the thought of her not believing him made his chest ache. Christ, it was driving him insane. He had to tell someone soon.

The last buzzer of Friday afternoon preceded a whooping cheer from everyone else in the class; a fitting full-stop to the end of what had felt like an incredibly long term. Noah couldn't remember ever feeling as tired. As he stood up and grabbed his pack from the back of the chair, with school over now Noah's thoughts turned to Sarah. She had still been haunting his dreams each night, with a growing urgency that she needed to see him. He hadn't been to the beach since he last saw her, but he planned to go that afternoon.

"...Noah Cooper! You haven't heard a word I've said, have you?" Mel's face came into focus; she was frowning.

"Sorry Mel, I was miles away. What did you say?" They were at their lockers pulling out books needed for the holiday's homework assignments.

"I asked if you wanted to go to the café... I've got something I need to talk to you about." She smiled in that secretive, annoying way only girls can. Noah sighed. He knew she'd reeled him in. For now at least, the beach would have to wait.

The café was a shabby little place on the corner of the road opposite the school. The two tables out the front overflowed with noisy school kids. Mel pulled open the heavy door which set off a bell somewhere in the back behind the counter. She gave a one fingered salute to a spotty, younger kid who had obviously made some comment about her she didn't appreciate.

"Bloody jumped-up seventh grader!" She turned around to Noah and rolled her eyes. He laughed. It was one of the many things he liked about Mel. She wouldn't take shit from anyone.

"We'll have two Cokes, thanks." Mel called out to the short, bald Italian behind the counter as the two of them slid into the seats of the back corner table. Noah's shoulders drooped with relief to see they had the place to themselves.

21

"No worries, love," said the friendly Italian. He brought the two glasses over to them. "Can I get you both something to eat?"

"I could seriously go a bacon sandwich!" Noah tutted in mock disapproval, and Mel suddenly looked guilty. "Oh, come on! Do you have any idea how hard it is to live with a pair of old hippy vegans who constantly tell you 'meat is poison'?" Noah laughed. He couldn't begin to imagine it. His dad insisted on meat every night of the week. Mel's parents ran the health shop in town, and the word 'meat' was definitely a four-letter word in their home.

"Come on then Mel, spill." Noah started to fidget. He didn't really have time for this; getting to the beach weighed heavy on his mind.

"Well, I don't know how to say this really, but has Nick said anything to you about well... you know, girls and stuff?" She picked fluff from the sleeve of her school jumper.

"No, can't say that he has." Noah felt his stomach flip over. "Why?"

"It's just that, well...." This was getting painful.

"You don't fancy him do you?" Noah blurted out the words. If only he could grab Mel's hand and find out precisely what she was thinking.

"Shit! Of course I don't, you dick. It's just that he has half the girls from our year trying to throw themselves at his feet and, well... he doesn't seem to be interested in any of them. Do you think he's gay?" Noah stared down into his glass and poked the ice-cubes with his straw.

"Well, he's not said anything to me, but I've got a feeling he has a crush on Mr. Sylvester. I don't know, Mel, maybe it's a phase."

"Shit, think of all those disappointed girls if he is!" She

giggled. "I couldn't care less if he is, but why hasn't he said anything to us? You think he would at least confide in us." She looked hurt. Noah knew what she meant. He felt rather stupid for believing she had feelings for Nick.

"I don't know, I guess he's embarrassed about it. Maybe you should talk to him." It was a cop out, but Noah figured their knowing would sound better coming from her.

They drank their Cokes in silence, each deep in their own thoughts.

The door opened and a crowd of older girls sauntered in, all five of them talking and laughing loudly. Noah glanced up and found himself eye to eye with Laura. He felt his face flush.

"Are you okay?" Jeez, Mel never missed a thing. He watched her devour half her bacon sandwich in one go, like some caveman who'd made his first kill in a month.

"Yeah, fine. I've got to get going though Mel; things to do..." he pulled on his shirt collar, very much aware of six pairs of eyes staring at him.

"What's the rush? It's Friday for God's sake." She sounded hurt; Noah couldn't look her in the eyes.

"Sorry, Mel, I've got things going on at the moment. It's complicated, but I'm hoping to have sorted a few things out by tonight. I'll give you a call later, okay? Maybe we can head to the mall tomorrow if you'd like." A love of shopping happened to be one of the many things they had in common.

"Okay, fine! Why is it I feel like everyone else has secrets except me?" Mel threw up her hands in mock despair. *Because you are right*, thought Noah guiltily, as he stood up to pay for the cokes and the sandwich.

*****

Noah pushed open the front door and threw his school bag down by the umbrella stand; he bent over trying to catch his breath. He'd jogged most of the way home wanting to get back before his mum got home from shopping. She did the shopping on Fridays and always had a million and one chores for Noah to do, as well. He didn't want to get caught up in that and risk not getting out to the beach.

"Just taking Jess for a walk," he shouted out to Kayla whose music was blasting from her room.

"Yeah, whatever," she called back. At least she'd heard him.

Noah grabbed the lead off its hook on the back of the door and Jess flew out from Kayla's room bringing out a cloud of cigarette smoke with her, and proceeded to waft it around the hallway with her madly wagging tail.

One of these days mum would catch her and Kayla would be in real trouble. Noah hoped he'd be around when it happened.

"Come on girl, let's get out of here." Jess led the way — she knew exactly where to go.

The clouds were pulling across the sky like a giant purple blanket – weather changed quickly on a peninsula; even more so than the rest of Victoria; the adage being 'If you don't like the weather — wait a minute!'

The huge thunderheads rolling in from the ocean were threatening. Noah could feel spots, but couldn't quite tell whether they were from the spray off the ocean or the beginning of a downpour.

Pausing at the top of the steps, he looked up the beach to the right. Sarah sat there in the same spot as though she hadn't moved since the last time he'd seen her. A wave of relief washed over him as he jumped the last two steps to the beach. Jess had joined her already; and lay comfortable next to this mysterious girl they'd only met once before.

"Well hello, Noah." She beamed at him. His stomach did a back flip as he mirrored her smile, genuinely happy to see her.

She straightened her legs out in front, pulling her dress over them, that same white dress she'd been wearing when he last saw her. Her slim feet were bare; the leather sandals lay where she'd kicked them off.

"Christ, aren't you cold?" Noah pulled off his jacket to give to her, but she shook her head.

"I don't feel the cold." There was mystery in her voice as she teased him again. "You've been avoiding me." Her deep, green eyes stared into his and ripped into his heart like they could squeeze every thought, every last secret from deep within him.

He sat down on the cold sand next to her, breathless.

"I've been busy. You know, school and stuff." He suddenly felt guilty for not seeing her sooner and angry with himself for caring.

"Don't you have to go to school while you're down here?"

"No, I don't. I used to go...I mean... my school's near the city." Sarah lowered her eyes, suddenly unsure of herself again.

"So, year eleven, is it? I'm in year ten. Jeez, I wish it were year twelve like my sister — I can't wait to leave that place." He knew he was waffling, avoiding what he really wanted to talk about with her. She nodded at him, and they fell into an awkward silence.

Noah's mouth filled with saliva, he swallowed nervously; certain she was waiting for him to speak.

"Sarah, I have to ask you something," now being as good a time as any.

"Were you on the beach, you know, the day..., well, the day

I saved that boy and had to be saved myself?" There. He'd finally said it.

She turned to him, and as she opened her mouth to speak, the rain started in buckets drenching the two of them instantly.

"Quick, come with me." Noah had to shout over the thunder that rumbled along with the lashing rain.

He grabbed her hand, but the flash that instantly filled the sky around them was lightning – nothing more. Noah saw no pictures when he touched her.

The thunder rumbled again, this time loud enough to send Jess running ahead of them. She knew where to find shelter, there was a compact cave in the side of the sandstone cliff around from where they'd been sitting.

It was drier inside than outside but only just.

Noah stood inches from Sarah in the confined space; his breathing heavy from the run. Why wasn't hers?

Her hair dripped onto her shoulders and down her back. A few stray strands had whipped across and were plastered to her cheek. Noah raised his hand slowly and brushed it away with his wet fingers. He had an overwhelming urge to kiss her.

As though she could read his thoughts, her eyes suddenly widened, she seemed to stiffen with panic and began to tremble. He still had her hand in his and realized how icy she felt. *Surely she's feeling the cold now?*

"It's okay. I won't bite." Her eyes softened as he used her words on her. He released her hand and took off his denim jacket, all the way this time. He placed it tenderly across her shoulders.

"Thank you."

They both sat down and Jess promptly shook herself as only dogs can, showering them both with more water.

"Jess!" Noah scolded, "Didn't you think we were wet enough?" They both laughed, each of them glad it had lightened the moment.

The cave was silent, a stark contrast to the sound of the torrential rain outside.

And then Sarah whispered an answer to the question he'd asked before the rain had interrupted him.

"Yes, Noah," She pulled her long hair from out of the jacket as she added, "I was there."

Noah opened his mouth to speak but didn't know where to start. He ran his hand through his wet hair. He looked at Sarah and then to the rain which fell a little steadier now. He wished he felt steadier too.

"I don't understand," he wiped his face with his sleeve as the water dripped from his hair.

"I was meant to be there, Noah."

"Do you know about 'the knowing'?" Noah had settled on this term for his strange, new ability. There had to be a connection, he was sure of it.

"You have no idea how long it took me to orchestrate that accident," she turned to him, her eyes unreadable.

"'Orchestrate the accident'? What the hell... do you mean you made all that happen?" The anger in his voice made her flinch.

"I needed help and, well, you getting a whack on the head was the only way you were going to be able to help." She looked apologetic.

"You needed help?" The words spat out of his mouth. "Why the hell didn't you just walk up to me and say 'Hi, I have a problem — can you help?' Wouldn't that have been fucking easier than making me nearly drown and ending up in hospital for four days?" He stood up now, his cheeks burning with fury.

"Sorry, Noah, but it was the only way I could come to you." Her voice was barely a whisper as she looked at him with wide eyes.

"I still don't get it. You mean you made all of that happen ...the boy, me, the driftwood, the surfer — everything? I could've died, for fuck's sake! Did you think about that before you set me up?" Noah clenched and unclenched his fists, desperate to stop the shaking.

"The 'knowing' as you call it — well, it's a gift from me, but it's something I could only give you in that place — the space which lies between life and death. It's something you're going to need to help me, Noah; and what's the point of having a gift if you don't share it?"

"A gift?" Noah's jaw clenched. His brain was beginning to feel like pulp. "What if I don't want to help? And I certainly don't want your damned gift. Do you think for one second seeing inside my family's heads and knowing their thoughts and feelings is a gift? What kind of witch are you to pass on to me these fucked up special powers?" He laughed maniacally. At least one thing was clear — he had his answer. She had been the catalyst to everything that had happened that day.

"Noah, calm down, please. I'll tell you everything." Sarah grabbed at his sleeve and coaxed him to sit.

He inhaled a deep, shaky breath, his head spinning, and reluctantly sat down next to her. He sure hoped she had some answers because he had a million and one questions.

Noah glared at her; his jaw still set tight. Sarah's face appeared paler than usual if that were possible.

"Okay. It was the last Friday night of the summer holidays, on this beach, in this cave," she closed her eyes and winced as though remembering was painful. Silent tears ran down her face as she continued.

"There was a man, quite a bit older than you are now. I thought he was kind of cool. I met him at a dance at the Civic Hall; he played drums in the band that played that night and we kind of clicked. I didn't want the night to end, so I agreed when he asked to walk me home. He told me the beach would be the perfect spot for seeing shooting stars, so I took his hand, and we walked down here." She wiped the tears from her face but continued.

"It was nice at first; he was funny and charming but then...." Noah reached for her limp hand. "It's okay, Sarah, go on."

"He started to get pushy, you know. And then when I tried to stop him he... he got so angry; he screamed at me and accused me of leading him on. I tried to get away....I felt so frightened, but he caught my arm and dragged me...dragged me here into this cave." The tears were flowing now.

Noah didn't think he wanted to hear any more.

"I struggled to pull away. I slapped him, but that made him even angrier. He pulled a flick knife out of his pocket and I'll never forget the look in his eyes. He was crazy, Noah. I had no doubt he intended to stab me with it! I tried to get away from him, I stepped back, and that's when it happened. I fell backwards and hit my head on a rock. And that was it — all over."

There were warning bells going off in Noah's head. "What do you mean 'all over'? What happened? I don't understand. Did he run away? Were you alright?" Something was gnawing away at his mind like a distant memory he couldn't quite reach. Something was very wrong.

"No, I wasn't alright at all." Noah felt the hairs stand up on the back of his neck as she looked into his eyes. "I'm dead."

Chapter Six

Electricity sparked inside the cave, or was it in Noah's head? Maybe he was a part of the storm — he could hear it, smell it, and feel it. He felt certain his head would explode into a huge blast of mixed senses; leaving his short life's memories scattered around the beach to be lost forever among the tiny grains of sand. Noah had no idea where to begin, he had a million questions formulating in his mind. Didn't everyone want to know about the one true mystery to man: what happens when we die?

"...but how? What...? Why...? Fuck!" Noah stuttered. He had no idea what to ask first. He couldn't believe it. She was a ghost, she'd seen the other side, had all the answers and Noah was desperate to know everything.

Sarah laughed — her eyes overflowing with the confidence of someone who knew all, and more importantly for Noah, was willing to share.

She told him everything it was. And she also told him everything it wasn't.

"At first there was a feeling of total tranquillity, I had absolutely no fear, Noah. I felt disconnected from my body and there was a corridor, but it was flooded with light, such a bright light – I had never seen a light so bright. At the end of the corridor was a door, such a beautiful, ornate, wooden door and then...I saw my grandparents! They had both died when I was little. I felt truly loved and safe. It felt so wonderful to be embraced by them both and reassured." She turned to Noah and he could feel the love radiating off her as she thought of her loved ones.

"I had a life review too. It was like watching a movie of all the good and bad things I'd done in my life. I didn't get the chance to live a long one, so it was fairly brief, but it made me feel so good about all I had done in my short years, even the bad things had been perfect lessons. I knew I was ready then and I felt no fear. The light was so, so beautiful I wanted nothing more than to feel its warmth and love and so I walked into it."

She paused briefly as though waiting for his next question.

"...so...when you entered the light...what did you see then?" Noah could hardly form the words he was so stunned by it all.

"There were no angels sitting on clouds, no pearly gates with some white bearded and robed father figure waiting with open arms, there's no stairway. The corridor melted away and suddenly I was in a garden. Oh, Noah! It was incredible! The colours of the flowers and the grass – I have never seen colours so bright, so vivid, so real! My door was still there, I walked towards it, but Nanna took my hand and shook her head to say 'no, not yet'. I thought my heart would burst with the pure love I felt." She was smiling through her tears now and her serenity was little comfort to Noah's disappointment.

"No, no, don't look like that! It's beautiful, Noah — really divine. It's like putting all the happy thoughts you've ever had all together. There's an essence – a source of all knowledge — we are all connected to and it's like going home; being one with it all again. I can't describe it." Tears were running in streams down her cheeks — Noah had never seen anyone look so happy.

"Everything we've learned here gets milked into the source so we can all have that one knowing. That total knowledge. It's bliss, Noah – pure bliss."

Noah sucked in a lungful of air, he felt light headed and no less confused than before. "So...it's more a feeling than an actual place?"

"This place..." she spread her arms out in front of herself and continued, "is a theme park, Noah. We choose the ride — and the people we want to ride with. We're here to use the lower five senses. It's the perfect place to see, feel, touch, taste and hear. It's a beautiful place. If we're lucky we might just remember the source – the divine; we might remember how to tap into that higher sense. If we can put the two together — wow! That's when we can really soar. For many though, remembering only comes at the end, with that final breath. But that's okay, too. We get to do it all over again." She reached up to Noah's face and wiped the tears from his cheeks — tears he didn't realise he'd shed.

"Did you have the choice to come back?" Noah yearned to touch her face, wipe her tears and feel what she was feeling. To know what she knew.

"Yes, Noah. I had the choice; we all get that choice, a chance to fix something we have been connected to in this lifetime. We can choose to send a message through a dream, keep watch over a loved one for a short while; some even choose to give someone a hard time — we can do any one of these things before we must move on again. But this was my choice, Noah, because of the connection between what has happened and what I have seen of the future. That source of knowledge is all that ever was – all that ever will be. And for now at least, I have that knowledge, too. Time is an illusion, Noah, it's been eleven years since it happened to me, but really it was only a moment ago. That knowledge tells me another life will be taken if I do nothing to stop it — I can't move on knowing that. And that's where you come in."

*****

"I'd rather be going to the mall — it's bloody freezing out there. Why on earth do you want to go to the beach?" Mel sat sulking on Noah's bed the following morning, aggressively picking fluff from her black-knit tights.

"Oh come on, it's school holidays, we'll go in the week. And anyway, maybe if you'd remembered to put a skirt on instead of that wide belt you're wearing, you wouldn't feel so freakin' cold!" Noah shoved his drawing book and pencils into his pack. He turned around and checked his hair in the mirror on his wardrobe door.

"Are we meeting someone there?" He could sense her watching him and suddenly felt self-conscious.

"Umm, hopefully, yes." He glanced up from fastening the bag and sheepishly grinned.

"You're kidding, right? Have you met someone?" Mel's eyes widened.

"Well kind of. She's 17, she's really cool and she needs my help."

This was beginning to feel really weird and Noah had no idea if it would even work.

Would Mel believe Sarah was even there, let alone a ghost?

He had stayed with Sarah on the beach for hours last night while the storm cleared and the sun set. He was still trying to come to terms with it all: the accident that wasn't an accident after all, the knowing and Sarah, Sarah being a ghost.

Noah knew exactly why Sarah was still here; the monster who had killed her eleven years ago in that cave had never been found and Sarah said there would be another murder.

She had to stop it — they had to find him, then she'd finally be at peace.

"Sorry Jess, you're going to have to stay home today — I'll take you out later." The poor, dejected dog slunk back into the kitchen as Noah and Mel closed the door behind them.

The fresh breeze blowing in from the ocean made Noah's face tingle, it wasn't an icy wind, but a reminder that autumn was well and truly here. The sun showed itself through the clouds; Noah looked up and closed his eyes for a second as though soaking up the last of its warmth.

"See? It's not cold — you might even be able to have a swim." He managed to dodge Mel's swipe, she soon gave up and pulled her jacket as far around herself as she could to warm up.

There were a few people on the beach, there always were on weekends. It would be a lot busier for the next two weeks. Tourists always flooded down for school holidays, it didn't seem to matter what the weather was doing.

"Is she here?" Mel was bouncing around like Jess always did when he brought her to the beach — it made Noah chuckle.

"Not sure, let's head down there and see." He led the way down the steps and silently prayed she would be. He turned his head right when they reached the bottom, and his smile was the answer to Mel's question.

"Does she know I'm coming?" Mel suddenly looked a little awkward.

"Don't worry, if she likes a knucklehead like me — she's bound to like you, too."

"Where is she?" Mel's head bobbed around like a chicken's as she desperately tried to get a look at Noah's new friend.

"She's sitting over there," Noah pointed ahead. Mel followed the line of his finger and frowned.

Mel couldn't see Sarah. Noah felt his heart sink, he had suspected that would be the case, but it would've made things infinitely easier if she'd been able to see her too.

This was going to be interesting to say the least.

Chapter Seven

"Hi Sarah," Noah smiled as he sat next to her – they really did feel like old friends now.

"I see you've brought a friend with you." Noah watched as Sarah appraised the girl at his side. Mel's hair was almost as dark as Sarah's, not as long and very curly in an unruly way. Noah could feel Mel's eyes on him, questioning.

"Okay, what's going on?" Mel stood with her arms akimbo and a frown on her face.

Noah and Sarah looked at each other and laughed— he had no idea how to begin.

"Sarah this is Mel, Mel this is Sarah. Now I know you can't see her, but maybe this will help..." Noah reached inside his pack and pulled out his sketch-pad and pencil.

Mel sat down next to him – and the three of them were silent as he put pencil to paper, expertly and quickly drawing a perfect likeness of his new friend.

"What the hell is going on here? Noah, you're scaring me!" Mel bit her lip, her eyes wide with fear.

"It's okay, Mel, This is Sarah." Mel seemed mesmerized but still looked completely confused. Noah glanced at her, and for a moment he had an overwhelming desire to sketch her, too.

Continuing to draw, Noah captured Sarah's eyes and wry smile perfectly.

"She's very pretty. Why can't I see her?" It was a logical question. Noah wondered if she thought he'd gone mad and had suddenly developed an imaginary friend.

"She's pretty, too," Sarah smiled at Noah in a knowing way; his cheeks burned, but he wasn't sure why.

"Sarah said you are too." This was weird. "Isn't there any way you can convince her you're here and I'm not going insane?" Noah put his pad down on the sand.

Sarah picked the book and pencil up causing Mel to gasp loudly. Sarah turned to a clean page and began to write; when she'd finished, she handed the pad to Noah who passed it on to Mel.

Hi Mel, it really is nice to meet you. I'm so sorry you can't see me – and don't worry, Noah hasn't lost his marbles, I really am here! I don't know how much Noah has said about me, I'm guessing not much from your understandable reaction, but the thing is... I'm dead. Only Noah can see me – and Jess (all animals can). I know this is going to be rather difficult, but I really hope we can be friends. *Sarah*

Noah watched Mel's cheeks turn crimson as she read the words on the page. She threw the pad onto the sand, like touching it burned her hands. She stood up again audibly gulping, Noah thought for a moment she was about to puke.

"How did you..? For Christ's sake, Noah! What the hell is going on?" Her voice had become high pitched and shaky.

"Look, Mel, I know this all seems a bit 'Twilight Zone', but it's real. Sarah's a ghost. She came to me through the accident so I can help her." Noah grabbed Mel's hand and gently coaxed her back down onto the sand.

"What do you mean, so you can help her?" Mel's eyes kept

shifting back and forth from Noah's face to the sketch pad.

"Sarah was killed on this beach eleven years ago. The guy who did it has never been caught, and Sarah knows it's going to happen again. We've got to stop him." Christ, he sounded like a nutcase. Mel's eyes were wide open, her mouth gaping in astonishment. Her hand was still in his. He felt her confusion, her amazing belief in him, and something else too. Was it jealousy? Noah felt his face heat up again as she stared into his eyes and he could read everything in hers.

"This is freaking me out. I have no idea what's going on but I believe you, Noah. How the hell could I not, after what I've witnessed. Sarah — wherever you are – you have one hell of a friend on your side, I'm happy to help in any way I can. I have no idea how we can though."

The three of them sat talking on the beach for the next two hours while Noah told Mel what had happened to Sarah. Mel listened silently; hands over her mouth as her eyes filled with tears.

Then Sarah closed her eyes and described every last detail of the man she'd spent her final moments alive with. Noah sketched quickly while she spoke and by the time they were done they had a pretty good idea of what he looked like.

"What was his name?" Mel spoke to the empty space next to Noah comfortably now.

"I never got a proper name. He told me his mates called him 'Rocky'. That was the only name I got." Sarah began to tremble. It obviously wasn't easy talking about the guy who had been responsible for her death.

Noah wrote the name under his sketch.

Mel scrutinized the drawing, her brows knotted together in concentration. Noah felt so relieved to have Mel on board. They had a murder to solve and the possibility of preventing one, too. Christ. They had one hell of a project for the school holidays!

*****

After reluctantly leaving Sarah on the beach, the two friends stopped at the little milk bar around the corner from Noah's place for hot chocolates to help them thaw out. They'd walked silently from the beach, both deep in thought. It had been quite some morning so far.

"How about starting at the library?" Mel wrapped her hands around the cup and blew into the steam rising off it.

"Well, we could look through back copies of the local paper for that year." Noah answered distractedly.

"What is it?" Mel took a sip and cussed as it burned her lips.

"It's the sketch. I don't know, but there's something familiar about that face." He took the pad out of his bag and placed it onto the table, not taking his eyes off the picture.

Sarah had told him Rocky's eyes where blue, really cold. His hair was blond but it might have been bleached, she wasn't sure of that. He didn't have any scars or moles she could remember seeing on his face.

Noah checked his watch; they weren't going to make it to the library today — it closed at 1pm and it was 12.30 already.

"Have you got much planned for the holiday?" Noah asked Mel, as she finally managed a mouthful of hot chocolate and ended up with a froth moustache. He smirked as she wiped her mouth with the napkin.

"As it happens, I've got no plans at all. What about Nick, though?"

"I haven't told him anything yet. We're not going to see much of him since he'll be helping out his dad and all." Noah tried to imagine what Nick would've made of all this. He'd probably think they were completely insane. Maybe it was a good thing he'd be too busy labouring for his dad's construction company.

"Okay, shall we meet at the library on Monday morning, then?" Mel looked suddenly excited as Noah nodded. *I guess we have to start somewhere.*

Chapter Eight

It sounded like World War III had broken out when Noah walked up the path to the front door later that day.

He smirked — could it be the day of reckoning for his sister? She'd gotten away with so much for so long he almost felt sorry for her. But when he walked in the house, his parents weren't ranting at Kayla, they were rowing with each other. He slammed the door louder than he needed to; his entrance created a moment of peace during the heated war.

His mum stood rigid in the hallway, hands on hips and chest heaving like she'd run a marathon. Her face was beetroot red from crying. His dad sat at the kitchen bench with his head in his hands.

"What's going on?" Noah dropped his bag immediately, and went to give his mum a hug.

He saw it all. She'd lost an envelope with money in it from her business — a lot of money. Beside herself with worry, she had instantly accused his dad of messing with her stuff on the desk in her office. He'd defended himself, naturally, and then threw insults her way about how awful her organizing skills were, and how she could've done a better job as a mother if she'd not started the damn business in the first place. My God, that had made her angry, he could feel her rage as she yelled at him – Noah could almost taste it. She'd even called him Thomas instead of Tom, but now all Noah could feel from his mum was utter desperation to find the missing envelope; otherwise she'd be up shit creek.

Noah flicked back the images he received from his mum; he could see her forgotten memories like rewinding on a remote control. That's when he saw it. Saw the envelope as it fell off the desk and landed behind a pile of manila folders stacked underneath. Noah shook his head at the vision; his Dad sure had a good point about her organizational skills.

He gently let go of his Mum and walked slowly into the office, dropped down on his knees and pulled the pile of folders out from under the desk — there it was. He picked up the envelope and could feel the wad of notes. He took a steadying breath before straightening himself and walking back out into the hall.

"Is this what you've lost?" He handed his Mum the envelope and smiling at them both, as his Mum stared open mouthed and his Dad gave one of his 'I told you so' looks, he turned around and walked off to his room.

Moments later there was a gentle knock on his bedroom door.

"Can I come in?" It was his mother.

Noah was lying on his bed studying the picture he'd drawn of Sarah when his mum walked in still holding the envelope.

"How did you..?" She looked puzzled as she waved the envelope at him, but happier at least.

"I saw this the other day — looks like a lot of money, Mum. When I saw how upset you looked, I put two and two together and well..." He hadn't taken his eyes off the picture and his mum moved closer to take a look over his shoulder.

"She's pretty. And she looks vaguely familiar, too. Who is she?"

Noah said, "She's someone who was murdered down at the

back beach eleven years ago, do you remember?"

"I do recall people telling us about the death of a young girl not long after we moved in — a bit of a nasty shock to be honest." She sat down next to him on the bed. "I thought we were moving to a lovely quiet place and to hear so soon about something like this happening was awful. Don't remember any of the details, though; eleven years is a long time ago and I'm lucky if I can remember what happened yesterday." Mum shook her head apologetically. Noah chuckled — she was right about that.

She smiled at him and touched his hand then, he was glad he'd been able to put a stop to the argument which would have gone on for days if he hadn't. She glanced at the picture and then asked, "Why do you need to know about her? Is it for a school project?" She looked hopeful; Noah never divulged any information about school.

"Yeah, Mel and I are going to work on it over the school holidays." Now she positively beamed. She stood up, and humming quietly, left Noah whose attention had strayed back to the picture.

He lay down the book and grabbed his laptop from off the desk; opening his browser, he typed in 'Sarah Nicholson' and clicked on 'search'. 12,800,000 results were found, yet absolutely nothing about her death. This would have to take good old-fashioned analogue research.

*****

The library buzzed with activity on Monday morning. Being the first day of school holidays, there were organized activities for already bored kids.

In the far right corner, where the picture books were propped up on low shelves for little children, one of the librarians strummed away on a guitar while singing nursery rhymes, along with the mothers of a few bewildered looking toddlers. A group of sixth grade boys were huddled around a gaming system, arguing over whose go it was next, while groups of giggling girls were checking out anything but the books. So much for a quiet place to research.

Mel glanced at Noah and smirked, "Want to go join them?"

Noah laughed sarcastically and continued over to the desk to ask about back copies of the local newspaper from December 2000 to March 2001. The bright and bubbly young assistant bounced past Noah and rushed off to a room down the back. She returned minutes later with a great stack of newspapers. Red in the face and out of breath, she plonked them down onto the counter, triumphantly.

"You're not allowed to remove these from the library," she announced with authority.

"Thanks." Noah grabbed half the pile and passed them to Mel, he took the rest of them and followed her to what he hoped would be a quiet corner of the library.

There were three tables with six chairs around each, and a row of more comfortable chairs lined up against the windows. An old man with a really bad comb-over sat at the last table, reading a newspaper, and a younger man sat by the window flicking through a book. Neither of them looked up as Noah and Mel dropped their large piles of papers onto the first table.

"Shouldn't be hard to find the initial report — it'd have to be front page news you'd figure." Noah sifted through the papers to see the front pages. And then he saw it.

He pulled out the paper and was faced with a half page picture of Sarah. Mel clambered around the table to sit next to him.

"Jesus, Noah, your sketch didn't do her justice — she's beautiful." Mel's voice whispered.

Noah couldn't think of any words as he studied the photo. He finally dragged his eyes to the headlines; Christ, the police weren't even sure it had been a murder — the newspaper had called it a 'tragic accident'. Noah was surprised at the anger welling up inside as he thought about that animal who had lived the last eleven years of his life with her blood on his hands.

"We've got to catch this bastard." He felt an utter sadness for not knowing this girl while she was still alive.

"We were only five then," Mel whispered, as though reading his mind.

They both read the article in silence. There were no details really; just that she had been staying with her family in their holiday home just as Sarah had said, and the police were eager to find any witnesses who had seen her that night, or anyone who was aware of her last movements.

Afterwards, Noah took the paper to the photocopier and took two copies each of the front-page headlines and the continued article on page three. There was a smaller picture there of Sarah and her parents. They looked happy together – the perfect family. Sarah was the image of her mother, and it suddenly struck Noah how the subject of her parents had never come up — they must have been to hell and back. He wondered where they were now and thought about what Sarah had said about making the choice she had made. It hit Noah like that plank of wood how important it was to find 'Rocky' — Sarah had given up the chance to see her folks one last time for this.

Mel suddenly jumped up; her eyes flashing like a light bulb had turned on inside her head.

"What about school?"

"What *about* school?" Into the first week of school holiday, school was the last thing Noah wanted to talk about.

Mel looked impatient, "This guy must have been a local if he knew about the cave down on the beach, and he had friends around him, so Sarah said. Surely he must have gone to our school."

Sarah had been pretty vague about his age — come to think of it; she hadn't known anything about him, really. He was older than she had been, that was clear — but how much older?

"It's difficult not knowing his age, but if we go back to 1998 we stand a good chance of him being at school then." Noah bit his lip but tried to sound more optimistic than he felt.

Five minutes later the pair of them poured over the yearbooks for Ryde High School 1998, they had located on the library shelves; both scrutinized every child's photo taken that year. Not one of the students looked anything like the sketch, and finally, Noah leaned back in his chair with a defeated sigh.

"He's not here, we're wasting our time. What next then, Mel?" His voice betrayed his disappointment as he wondered how they were going to find this needle in a haystack.

"Well, don't know about you, but I'm getting hungry." Mel tidied the papers and books into a neat pile to hand back to the librarian.

Noah agreed, although looking at Mel he wondered how anyone could eat as much as she did and still manage to stay so slim. She looked good; he found himself following her with his eyes as she sauntered over to return the books. *Christ, she must've sprayed those jeans on.*

She turned around then as though she knew he would be watching her, and Noah snapped his head away embarrassed he'd been caught looking. When she walked back to the table she flicked her hair in that confident way he'd seen her do before when she felt pleased about herself. Noah couldn't look at her for fear of blushing.

Mel slapped him on the shoulder, "Come on then — let's eat."

He could feel from her touch how pleased she felt about herself. Noah had been checking her out; it made him feel kind of weird, not a bad weird though — he also knew exactly what she wanted to eat.

"Right then, two chicken dinners from Hungry Rooster's coming right up." He stood up and grabbed his bag; now it was his turn to feel cocky as he glanced sideways at Mel's gaping mouth.

"How did you...?" But Noah had already walked out the door.

Chapter Nine

The hunt went nowhere for the next two days. Noah couldn't stop staring at the picture of Sarah with her parents. He wondered how they'd lived without knowing what had really happened to their daughter for all these years; he hadn't been able to think of anything else, it wasn't till his mobile rang on Thursday morning he realised he'd been neglecting his other friend.

"What's up?"

"Noah, can I come round?" Nick didn't sound his usual confident self.

"Sure you can. You alright?" Noah chewed on his lip. Something was wrong.

"I'll be there in five."

Noah ran a hand through his hair and jumped out of bed. He wasn't even dressed and there were papers and notes strewn all over the room. He frantically attempted to tidy them up. Normally he couldn't care less about the state of his room when friends came round, but he didn't want to leave anything around that would attract questions. He had a niggling feeling in the pit of his stomach he was trying to ignore.

The doorbell rang as he pulled on his jeans.

"Noah!" His mum shrilled from down the hall, "Nick's here!" She disappeared into her office as Noah walked out to meet his friend at the front door.

Nick's face looked gaunt and blotchy and his eyes were red; something was very wrong.

"What's wrong, mate?" Noah put an arm around Nick's shoulder not wanting to wait for an answer that might not give him the truth. The flash appeared almost invisible to him now as Nick's memories and emotions emerged into Noah's mind.

He could see Nick standing in the huge tiled hallway of his home, while Nick's father stood inches away, craning to look up at his young son; the older man's face was contorted with anger and his eyes black. Nick's dad was going ballistic; spitting out words so quickly and loudly in Greek. Noah couldn't make out what the hell he was saying, but it was pretty damn clear his words were full of hate for his only son. He saw him pointing at the door and pushing Nick forcefully towards it — all the while; Nick's tiny mother was pulling at her husband's arm, crying hysterically. It was a horrific scene and Noah fought back tears for his friend, as the two of them walked into his room.

"Come on then – spill." Noah mentally shook his head in the hope of clearing the images he had seen. He sat backwards on his chair at the desk while Nick slumped onto the bed. When he looked up there were tears running down his friend's cheeks.

Noah swallowed hard but the lump in his throat wouldn't budge.

"He threw me out." Nick wiped his face quickly with the back of his hand and continued.

"I've got these magazines, see," he looked up at Noah who laughed briefly.

"Mate, what sixteen year old *hasn't* got those magazines?"

"No, not that kind of magazine; different ones I'd got off

50

the net..." he looked away for a moment and Noah wasn't sure he would continue.

"Go on," he moved next to Nick on the bed.

"...magazines... of men, Noah." He looked up at his friend and then the tears really started to come.

"Are you...?" It killed Noah to watch his friend so painfully open his heart when he already knew everything.

"Shit Noah, I don't know. Maybe...well, yes." The poor guy sounded so confused.

"Jeez, your dad must have gone off his nut." Noah laughed, wanting desperately to convince his friend that this wouldn't change a thing between them.

"Yeah, he did as it happens. Said no son of his was going to be...you know... and told me to get out."

"Well, you can stay here as long as you need to," Noah slapped him on the back as Nick's face brightened with the relief of unloading his burden.

"...don't think you'll be sharing my bed though, will you mate." Noah thought a joke would help to lighten the moment, but Nick's laugh was strained.

"Nah, you're not my type!"

Noah couldn't help admire his friend's strength. He couldn't begin to imagine how hard all of this had been for Nick.

"Don't worry, mate. I'm sure he'll come round. You know how much he cares about you, and I bet he'll be getting a hard time from your mum about this too." She may have been a tiny, quiet woman, but Nick's mum could certainly be manipulative when she wanted something. Noah had witnessed it many times before.

While in the kitchen making ham rolls for the two of them,

Noah stopped briefly to text Mel; she needed to know Nick had confessed what she'd suspected. She also needed to know things had changed and they were going to have to include Nick in on their project. Noah felt lighter; he hadn't meant to keep everything from Nick — it had just kind of ended up that way.

His phone beeped as he put the butter away in the fridge. She was coming over.

"I don't know what to say." Nick had listened to Noah and Mel in silence while they had told him about Sarah and the accident, about her being a ghost and how she'd been killed in that cave at the beach and her killer had never been found. He looked completely dumbfounded.

"Yeah, and you thought what you had to tell us was newsworthy!" Mel sat next to Nick on the bed. She seemed as relieved as Noah that he had finally come out. All of that was forgotten now they had shared their news.

"Well, at least we have no secrets between us anymore." Mel grinned at the two of them. Noah suddenly felt a heavy weight in the pit of his stomach. He still hadn't told them everything; he didn't want to keep it to himself any longer.

"There's something else." His hands felt sweaty and he could feel Mel's hazel eyes burning into him, but he couldn't look at her.

"...after the accident there's been something different about me." He still couldn't look at Mel, he focused on Nick instead.

Nick opened his mouth as though wanting to say something smart but thought better of it.

"Sarah gave me this gift...I can see what's in people's minds ... if I touch them, or they touch me." He looked up then; not sure what reaction he would get from his two best friends.

"What are you saying? Do you mean you can see what someone's thinking?" Nick looked completely impressed and more than a little bewildered by Noah's new skill, but Mel sat in silence on the bed, her face unreadable. He wished he could use his gift on her to understand exactly what she was thinking right now.

"Well, yeah, I can see pictures — you know, of what's happened to the person recently or anything they are thinking of and well, I can tell their emotions, too. It's crazy. There's a blue flash in my head, it used to hurt, but not anymore and then it's like watching a DVD. You know the guy at the milk bar? He's in love with the hairdresser at the shop next door — has been for the last two years – and can't bring himself to ask her out. I sensed his feelings when he gave me my change the other day. It's crazy! And you don't want to know what Mr. Kippling and Mrs. Mason do at school during their lunch break!" He raised his eyebrows in a knowing way at Nick, desperate to lighten the stormy mood he could feel oozing from Mel.

"Sarah told me I had to have the accident so she could give me this power; so I could help her."

"You've got to be shitting me!" Nick shook his head, he looked dazed. "Do you have any idea how powerful this is? What you could do with such a gift?"

Mel jumped off the bed, her eyes flashing with anger. "It's true isn't it?" Her cheeks were flashing too. "Why the hell didn't you tell me this before? You've been hiding this information for as long as you could to use it on me?" She looked hurt — really hurt – and Noah felt like a heel for not telling her sooner.

"I'm sorry, Mel. It's not like that." His words sounded small.

53

"That's how you knew what I wanted to eat when we were at the library; you knew about Nick, too, didn't you? What else do you know about you might care to share with us? My god! You could know everything you'd ever want to know about anyone! Isn't that some kind of breech of people's privacy? As for me and Nick, shit, we don't even need to talk to you anymore, all you have to do is slap us on the shoulder and it's all there for you isn't it?" Jeez, she was really mad now. Her hands were making fists, Noah was afraid she wanted to punch something...or someone.

"It's not something I'm happy about, you know. I didn't know how to tell you — I thought you'd think I had gone mad." Even to Noah it sounded like a feeble excuse.

"Oh, and having a ghostly girlfriend was okay to share with me but this...this wasn't?" He knew he'd messed up; it was going to take a lot to make up for this.

"Well I think it's cool. What I'd give to know what other people were thinking — it's one heck of a super power!" Nick tried valiantly to prevent the major fight brewing between Noah and Mel.

"I'm sorry I didn't tell you sooner, I really am." He directed his apology at Mel and hoped she could understand. "And at the moment, it looks to be our only weapon to help with this murder case."

Chapter Ten

Even with the gift, Noah still had no idea how they were supposed to find this person without a proper name or anything else to go by. But at least there were three of them to put their heads together now. Whether they could come up with anything remained to be seen.

After filling Nick in on everything that had happened since the accident, the first thing they were going to have to do was take him to meet Sarah. In fact, Nick had insisted on it.

The three of them, along with Jess, walked down to the beach; Nick chatted constantly the whole way there – which was probably a good thing because Mel shuts up when she sulks, and Noah couldn't speak for the big ball of guilt stuck in his throat.

On the sandy path down to the steps they passed a surfer who was still wet from the waves, his wet-suit at half-mast and sand stuck to his bare feet like some weird pair of shoes. He smiled at the three of them as he said, "G'day!"

Mel's head swivelled around to follow his buff body with an appreciative eye and something stirred in Noah's stomach that made him feel something he'd never felt before.

"He's too old for you; must be 30 if he's a day." He mumbled under his breath as he stomped past her towards the steps. He glanced around and realized Mr. Surfer with a six-pack's impressive body had been enough to stop Nick in his tracks, too.

Noah swore. "Are you two coming?" He started to wish he hadn't told Nick anything.

*****

Nick fell absolutely spellbound by Sarah; it didn't seem to matter he couldn't see her. She wrote him a message on Noah's notebook which completely blew Nick's mind even more than the same trick had freaked out Mel. He had a million and one questions to ask.

"What's it like after...you know?" Nick ran his hands through his hair. Noah couldn't remember the last time he'd seen him look so mystified.

"Did anyone meet you? Did you go through a tunnel of light? Were there angels?" Nick reeled them off one after the other, and while he couldn't see Sarah, he obviously had absolutely no doubt she existed.

"Okay, Nick, enough with the questions, already." Noah sounded far sharper than he'd intended to. He still felt rather agitated, his irritation grew more with having to repeat everything Sarah said. His gums ached painfully adding to his irritability. Nick opened his mouth again but clearly thought better of it.

"Right then Sarah, you need help — we're all here to help but we're going to need more to be going on with than a nick-name and a sketch. Is there anything else you can remember about him that you haven't told me yet?"

No one spoke for a moment — they seemed to sense Sarah needed time to re-live those last moments, yet neither of them could possibly understand how difficult it must be for her.

Noah watched her face intently as she stared into the sand, until her face shot up suddenly, her eyes wide.

56

"There was something else! I can't believe I'd forgotten. He had a tattoo, nothing unusual really, on his back between his shoulders – he wore a singlet; I saw the tattoo when he took his jacket off. It was a bird — a black bird with its wings outstretched."

Noah grabbed his sketch pad and pencil, his hands shaking slightly. He passed it to Sarah and asked gently, "could you draw it?"

Nick and Mel both looked puzzled; it was easy to forget they couldn't hear Sarah. He told them about the tattoo but wouldn't take his eyes off the picture Sarah drew on the pad. It wasn't a perfect picture — clearly, drawing wasn't her thing; but clear enough for Noah to see when she'd shaded it in that the tattoo was more than a little familiar. He just couldn't quite work out why.

Chapter Eleven

"I wish Sarah could come with us. I don't understand why she can't move away from the beach. I figured a ghost would be able to go anywhere they'd want to, you know, apparate or something." Mel looked a little left out sitting on the chair at Noah's desk, while the two boys were doing a pretty good job of thrashing the life out of each other on a video game.

"She's a ghost, Mel. Not a witch." Nick spoke without moving his eyes off the screen.

Noah felt a pang of guilt again as he remembered he'd still not asked Sarah about her parents.

He glanced around at Mel and laughed when he saw her pout. Her forehead had two deep furrows like tram-lines — she still looked cute. He felt so glad she was talking to him again.

"I'll let you play the winner if you want; it's going to be me anyway," said Noah. His multi-tasking skills weren't the greatest, and talking to Mel had distracted him from the game. Nick's player took full advantage and delivered the last fatal blow. Noah cussed. She'd got his full attention now.

"I know what you mean, Mel. I wonder what she does when we're not there. I hope we can help her — you know, if we don't, she might be stuck in limbo forever." Noah shivered. It was something he'd been thinking about often.

"I think we need to look at those school yearbooks again, Noah."

Noah rolled his eyes. "We've been there, done that; no joy."

"Maybe because we assumed he was still at school in 1998. If he had a tattoo he must have been more than 18 and most likely not at school." Mel moved from the chair onto the bed next to Noah.

Nick spoke, but his eyes were still fixed on the game he now played solo. "Not necessarily, Mel. You can still get a tattoo at 16 as long as you've got permission from your parents."

"Okay, fair enough, but I reckon this guy had already left school and probably a long time before. What if we check the yearbooks from about five years before then – what do you think?" She looked at Noah, hopefully.

"You've got a point. How about we head there now? Nothing much else going on and I don't feel like getting my ass kicked again by Jackie Chan here. If Mum thinks it's for studying she'll definitely give us a lift."

Noah was right. His mum was more than happy to oblige, more likely happy for the excuse to escape the office. In less than twenty minutes the three of them were rifling through the yearbooks of the two high schools in the area for the years Mel suggested.

The library buzzed with activity. Kids up to a certain age did not understand the concept of whispering. Due to some sort of craft work going on, the whole place stank of the heady smell of glue.

They picked a book each and Noah placed the sketch of their man on the table in front of them. Nick scrutinized it quietly for a while before he opened his book.

For the next half hour, the three of them were the only source of silence in the whole library — all of them deep in concentration. And then, just as Noah began to accept they were barking up the wrong tree, Mel screamed so loud a brief moment of silence followed from the rest of the library. The buzzing returned once everyone realized nobody had suffered from the mother of all paper cuts.

She jumped up off her seat with so much force the chair fell over behind her. "I've got him! I've got him!" Mel did a celebratory dance and waved the book around while Noah and Nick desperately tried to grab a look.

There he was, just like the sketch in Noah's pad, only younger looking. It was eerie to see a real photo of him. The sketch didn't do him justice; he had shifty eyes and a cruel mouth and his demeanour was one of conceited confidence in his apparent good looks. Noah's stomach churned with the strange familiarity he had felt looking at the sketch. He hated him. No-one should look that cocky at that age — he was in year 10, the same as they were now. But it was the name that left them all speechless.

Robert Sylvester.

"Oh come off it," Nick snapped. "Sylvester's a common enough name. It's a coincidence that's all." Obviously Nick did not like the implication Noah and Mel had instantly connected this villain with his adored biology teacher.

"Take a good look, Nick — think shorter darker hair and throw in a few wrinkles and ...voila!" Noah's stomach did a flip as Nick flinched at his words. "You've got to admit, there's a definite resemblance there." Noah battled with some pretty strange emotions. He could see how much this hurt Nick, but he really needed his friends to be on the same page.

"It's got to be him — look!" Mel said quietly to Nick. "He hasn't changed that much in all these years has he?" She touched Nick on the arm; she obviously didn't think she needed to convince Noah.

"There's only one way to know for sure," Noah placed a hand on Nick's shoulder and tried to do the same with Mel who ducked away from his touch. Trying to ignore the mixed emotions he could see from Nick and the hurt he felt from Mel's reaction, he said what he knew they were thinking as well.

"We've got to see if he's got that tattoo."

*****

The ride home in his mum's car would have been silent if it hadn't been for his mum's incessant chatting. The only other sound came from Nick's phone, which beeped the arrival of a new text message. He struggled to pull it out of his black, skinny jeans' pocket, glanced at the screen and raised his eyebrows. He turned it off, shoved it back into his pocket and didn't utter a word for the rest of the journey.

Noah knew it must have been his mum, and when they climbed out of the car at Noah's place he managed to brush his arm against Nick's. Noah hardly noticed the blue flash, but the images in his mind confirmed his previous thoughts.

"Why don't you give her a call?" Noah said. The words were whispered so his mum wouldn't hear. "She's bound to be worried about you."

Nick looked down at his feet, noticeably awkward. "Yeah, I guess I should. I couldn't care less what *he* thinks, though." Noah knew this was a big, fat lie. He left Nick alone as he followed his mum and Mel back inside the house.

"I need to think." Mel's brow showed those tram-lines again. They'd all been trying to digest the information they had seen in the library; and he knew exactly what that meant.

"Okay, I'll fix us something to eat then and leave you to it."

He wanted to check in with Nick and find out how things were for him on the home front. It didn't take long.

Nick strolled in with the smallest hint of a smile on his face and his eyes shiny with tears.

"How're things?" Noah busied himself with making lunch.

"They miss me. He's calmed down apparently and mum said he didn't mean all the things he said. They want me to come home so we can patch things up." He looked thrilled and Noah couldn't help but feel the same.

"That's great news, mate. You know you can stay here anytime you need to. Are you heading home now? You could at least have something to eat first, and besides — Mel's *thinking!*"

"Oh, this I've got to see!" Nick beamed as he grabbed a plate of salad wraps, and they both headed for Noah's room.

Mel had managed to find a small patch of clear carpet; she had thrown her boots and socks off under the desk and was standing on her head, her body in a perfect straight line with her eyes closed in total concentration, she didn't even sway when they walked in. Noah couldn't help notice how each of her bright pink painted toenails, which were pointing straight up to the ceiling, had a tiny daisy painted on and he marvelled at how long that must have taken her to do.

The two boys sat on the bed. Noah couldn't take his eyes off her upside down face. Mel's parents had taught her yoga from a very young age; in fact, she'd even tried showing Noah how to do the sun salutation one sunny Saturday when they were both six. She didn't get far; when she showed him how to do dog head down he'd toppled over on top of her in a fit of giggles. There was something quite amusing about sticking your bum up into the air. Noah had an overwhelming desire for her to show him again now; he would definitely be so much more attentive than he had been back then.

"Okay, I've got it!" she said as she finally stood the right way up again.

· She grabbed a salad wrap, peeked inside, frowned at the lack of meat and continued. "I corner Mr. S after class to get his advice on tattoos, you know, like I want to get one, and you hang around putting your books away then you can use your special powers by brushing past him or something, and hopefully, he'll be thinking of his tattoo."

It wasn't brilliant, but it was better than nothing. They couldn't really do much more until the start of the new school term on Monday week.

"Wouldn't it be easier to ask him if he has one?" Nick looked a little hurt he had no part in the scheme.

"But what if he was ashamed of it? He might choose to lie about having one. It's better to get him onto the subject and let Noah do the rest," said Mel as she hopped on one foot while putting her boot back on.

Noah was still struggling with his emotions though. None of this felt right somehow. Mr. Sylvester had always been a respectable teacher and tarnishing the name of a man they all admired in one way or another wasn't going to make anyone feel good. The tattoo was their only connection. It had to be the answer.

Chapter Twelve

School holidays have a way of flying by, unless for some unusual reason, you need them to. For Noah, the last seven days had dragged like the week before Christmas did when you were a kid.

Monday morning arrived grey and wet. The rain was slow but relentless and didn't help lift Noah's mood. He had only just made the bell, so didn't get to catch up with Mel or Nick before classes began. Biology was the first lesson for the day and Noah hoped the cramp in his stomach would settle down once they had some answers.

Mr. Sylvester breezed into the classroom, his usual bright, cheery self – how could anyone be so optimistic on a Monday morning?

Noah couldn't look at him — he thought about the sketch from Sarah's description, the tattoo and the photo from the yearbook they'd seen at the library. The pieces should have fitted together perfectly, but it still didn't feel right.

As luck would have it, the subject they were studying was sun, skin and cancer. Nice, but at least it could be a legitimate lead to questions on tattoos.

Noah glanced across the room at Mel who looked back at him and gave him encouraging thumbs up.

It felt like the lesson dragged on forever. Performing an

evaluation of test moles and providing a description of cancer in terms of cell biology was yawn-worthy stuff. Besides, Noah found it difficult to concentrate on anything.

Eventually the buzzer went followed by the usual mad rush out the doors. Noah looked across at Mel who was rummaging for something inside her bag, a stalling tactic while waiting for the other students to leave. He gave Mr. Sylvester a side-wards glance and could see the teacher about to walk out, Mel had spotted it too.

"Oh, Sir, can I ask you for some advice?" Mel called out to him from the back of the classroom as she scrambled to put everything back into her bag.

Mr. Sylvester stopped inside the doorway — perfect. Noah would have to squeeze past them to get out. He stooped over to adjust his perfectly tied laces and watched the two of them from under his desk. He couldn't quite hear what Mel said, but Mr. Sylvester was shaking his head. His reply must have been amusing because Mel laughed, louder than Noah thought necessary.

It was clearly his cue.

He grabbed his bag and made for the door, mumbling, "...'excuse me", as he pushed past the teacher and waited for the flash: it came fast and bright — no pain, Noah had grown used to it now.

He shuffled along the corridor and waited outside the art room. He didn't really need to hear what Mel had to say as she rushed up to him. He knew the answer already.

"Nope, no tattoos, Noah. He absolutely hates them." She flicked a curly piece of hair off her face and said the words Noah didn't need to hear. "Looks like we're back to square one."

"I knew it wasn't him!" Nick looked the picture of relief

when he caught up with the two of them at lunch, and Mel had filled him in on the news.

The three of them were seated on one of the rickety, old benches wrapped around a huge, old gum tree to the right of the hall.

"It doesn't make sense though — the photo, the name — how could it not have been him?" Mel queried as she munched on her salad.

Noah, overwhelmed with disappointment, couldn't think of anything to say. All that work for nothing and poor Sarah was no closer to being able to finally move on.

With his lunch uneaten on his lap and not much of an appetite, Noah watched the comings and goings around them while the other two continued the conversation.

Two younger girls walked past; one slightly older than the other; both of them chatted excitedly about something. Noah glanced from one to the other; the younger had short, spiky dark hair and was what his mum would call 'pleasantly plump' while the older one stood a foot taller with a very slim frame, her hair was the colour of corn, but their faces were almost identical.

Noah jumped off the bench, knocking his lunch box onto the floor where his sandwich spilled out everywhere. He couldn't believe he'd been so stupid.

"They're brothers!" He called out so loudly the two girls stopped briefly and stared at him.

Nick and Mel looked completely puzzled until she followed Noah's line of sight, spotted the two sisters and realized exactly what he meant.

"Oh my God, you're right!" In all the excitement, Mel forgot she still had a mouthful of salad — most of which landed on top of Noah's sandwich.

"Just do the math; it doesn't add up does it? Mr. S would have to be in his mid 30s, and there's no way he's that ancient."

Nick, as always, took a little longer to catch on. His face was a picture of total confusion as he looked from one to the other.

"Keep up, Nick! Don't you get it? Mr. S has to have a brother. It's the only thing that makes sense." Mel grinned like an idiot at Noah and his mood lifted instantly.

They were back in the game.

*****

It was great news, but how the hell were they going to find out about Mr. Sylvester's brother?

Mel, who seemed to get on rather well with the handsome teacher — much to Noah's annoyance — said she would go and ask him the next time she spotted him in the corridor.

That hadn't stopped Noah from Googling Mr. Sylvester's name for the last ten minutes on his laptop.

He came up with diddly-squat; zip, nothing. The guy has no digital fingerprint whatsoever, Christ; he doesn't even have a Facebook page. Maybe it would be easier to let Mel ask.

Noah really needed to see Sarah. It had been nearly a week since he had seen her, and the guilt was driving him mad. Besides, he missed her. He felt like a much better person when he was around her.

He glanced at the time on his laptop, five o'clock and almost dark outside. The rain continued in waves, a few seconds of nothing then a raging torrent as though God had turned some giant tap on and off for a laugh. It would have to wait. Noah didn't feel much like getting drenched tonight. He stared gloomily at the pile of homework sitting on the edge of his desk; it was about as inviting as a nun's 21st birthday party.

Just as he thought he needed to come up with the perfect excuse not to do it, there was a knock on his bedroom door.

"Hey, champ. Want to come watch this new movie with me?" His dad waved a DVD in his face; the latest action blockbuster.

Noah took one last fleeting look at the pile on his desk and nodded, "Couldn't think of anything else I'd rather do!"

"Do you think Kayla would be interested?" his dad asked. There had been a time when she would have loved these films as much as Noah. His dad knocked on her bedroom door and opened it ajar, just enough for a projectile cushion to fly through which smacked him in the stomach. "GO AWAY!"

"I'd say that was a 'no', Dad." Noah said as he tried opening the door a little wider while his dad walked off with a shrug towards the lounge. He managed to grab a quick look at his sister. Her face looked like some freaky panda, her black eye make-up running down her cheeks from what must have been a massive sob-fest.

"You okay?" Noah asked with genuine concern but his sister stormed towards the door, pushed his arm out of the way, and slammed it shut without another word.

That touch was all Noah needed to see exactly what had made his sister so moody. She had been ceremoniously dumped by her weirdo boyfriend. And apparently it happened because she had refused to sneak a bottle of booze into her bag and walk out of the bottle shop without paying for it for him. Noah saw her standing alone, and could feel her heartbreak, as she watched her boyfriend walk away.

Noah desperately wanted to march back in there and tell her she was better off without that creep. He also wanted to say how cool he thought she was to not stoop to her low-life boyfriend's way of thinking, but that look on her face made him think better of it.

Nearly two hours later, Kayla hadn't ventured out of her room; Noah stood in front of her bedroom door with a huge bowl of buttered popcorn and knocked softly. "It's me, Kay. I've got you some popcorn." She couldn't say no to that.

He was right, she couldn't.

She pulled the door open slowly and allowed him in. They might have had their differences, but Noah hated to see his sister so miserable.

"He's not worth it, you know." Noah scooped a handful of popcorn and shoved the whole lot into his mouth.

"How do you know it's about a guy?"

"Oh come on; when we were kids you could just about take your leg off at the knee and not cry. But you've got a soft heart, you even cried at the end of 'Finding Nemo' for God's sake!" Noah chuckled at the memory.

She looked up at him — her face all blotchy and swollen — she almost smiled.

"Yeah, but so did Nick," she giggled, and Noah knew she would be all right.

Chapter Thirteen

The rest of the week remained uneventful. Mel didn't get her chance to ask Mr. Sylvester about his brother because he had been away from school. A sub teacher stood in to take his lessons.

As frustrating as that was, it wasn't as frustrating as the monotonous rain that drizzled continuously every single day. Noah couldn't stop thinking of Sarah; the longer he went without seeing her, the more he worried she would think they had forgotten her.

The end of the final period couldn't come quick enough on Friday. Especially after what Noah had learned about one of the students that morning. The usual mad rush to grab last minute books and the corridor heaved with noisy pupils. One younger boy pushed into Noah's back as he tried to navigate through the chaos.

"Sorry." His mutter was barely audible.

"Don't do it mate! Seriously, things will get better!" The words popped out of Noah's mouth before he realised he'd spoken them and not just thought them. The slim, blond haired boy stopped in his tracks and now stood open mouthed, his eyes questioning Noah.

"S..s..sorry?" The boy found his voice, but only just. Noah stuck his hands in his pockets, uncomfortably aware other kids were now paying attention.

"Umm...you're Kelly Morris's brother aren't you?" The boy nodded in apparent shock someone should have noticed him.

"She talks about you all the time." Noah hoped that little lie wouldn't come back to bite him on the ass.

"She says you're pretty damn good at War of Horror...you finished the whole game in four hours!" Raising his eyebrows and nodding enthusiastically to the gathered audience, Noah was really getting into the role.

"Freakin' awesome work, mate! I could do with some tips on getting past the third mission if you ever have time to talk..?"

The young boy's expression changed from one of shock to one of blushing pride as impressed whispers rippled through the crowd.

"Sure thing! It's dead easy really. I'd be happy to help. I could meet you after school if you'd like?" He positively beamed now as the buzzer sounded for first period.

"Cool! Thanks, Carl. See you outside the front entrance after last bell." Noah turned away and some how made his way to class. His hand quivered as he touched the door handle, he paused for a moment to compose himself before heading into class.

That young kid's head had been full of one thing and he'd been pretty damn serious about it too. Suicide.

Noah waited for Carl outside school, as it happened, so had a few others. And when they saw Carl walking through the gates with a little more confidence than he'd had that morning, the other kids jumped at him with questions about the game. Before long, Carl was engrossed in conversation with some new friends and Noah, trusting that he wouldn't be missed, threw up his hand at Carl with a 'I'll catch you another time' glance and left them to it.

*****

Noah woke up early Saturday morning with absolute relief to see the rain had stopped. Their local market day had arrived and his dad was always keen to get there early. His mum didn't like the trash 'n' treasure market; she believed one man's trash was, well, trash. Noah thought she had a good point really. Many times his dad would come home with a boot full of useless stuff that would end up gathering dust in the shed. Other times he would end up with a car full of plants for his beloved garden and then he would have to spend hours trying to work out exactly where he could squeeze them in.

Noah flashed his teeth at his reflection in the bathroom mirror and wiped at them with his finger. Mel would be joining them today. She needed to shop for a present for her dad.

"Are you ready then?" Dad called from the kitchen.

Noah walked out with rucksack on his back and his dad let out a very loud wolf whistle that brought Jess running from the other room.

"Who are we trying to impress today, then?" His dad's eyes sparkled as he teased his son because he had had a shower, combed his hair for once and put on a clean pair of jeans.

Tom slapped his son on the back and handed him the car keys as the pair of them headed out. Noah stopped dead in the doorway and face palmed. His dad's mind was on one thing this morning as they walked out to the car; Noah was given a timely reminder it was his mum's birthday tomorrow and he had completely forgotten all about it. It looked like Mel would not be the only one looking for a present today.

By the time they had picked up Mel and parked up in the jetty car park the sun reflected liquid gold across the bay. It was glorious to see after so long, but its autumn warmth had little effect on the muddy, sodden foreshore where the market stalls were already mostly set up. People squelched in both directions and before long the aisle in the middle of the two rows of stalls turned into one giant mudslide.

Noah's dad had already disappeared as Mel helped Noah set up his two fold-up chairs and sandwich board sign — 'Artist drawn portraits while you wait — $50'.

Noah could hear a group of girls, familiar giggles and chattering. It was Laura Penrose and her hangers on. They all looked like they were going to a club; high heels, short dresses and enough make-up to scare a small child. He heard Mel 'tut'.

Then just as they were directly in front of Noah one of the girls took a tentative step but left her shoe behind in the mud. She looked back — horrified, it was Laura.

Noah grabbed the muddy shoe and handed it to a very embarrassed Laura; she may well have been blushing, but he couldn't tell with all that paint on her face.

"Thanks, Noah," she whispered. She smiled sweetly as she took the shoe, their fingers touching briefly. It was a shame that smile wasn't for him. He could feel her excitement; the thoughts in her head were all about meeting up with her new boyfriend. Thoughts so steamy they created a stir in Noah's jeans. *Fuck me! Those breasts are enormous!* Noah found it impossible to look anywhere else. He watched her as she briefly took in the words on his sandwich board before she sauntered off with as much dignity as someone who had left their shoe behind in the mud could muster.

"You'll catch flies like that." Mel had stopped laughing and now stood with her hands on her hips looking more than a little annoyed.

"I'm gonna leave you to it. See if I can't find something suitable for a 40 year old hippy," and she was gone.

The morning moved pretty slowly. Nothing worked better

for business than having someone sit with him for a portrait. People would stop and check out his work to see if what he was sketching was anything like the person in front of him. He was good. That was usually all it took. A successful day would provide five or more customers; if the weather cooperated, or it was a long weekend and tourists were aplenty, he'd get twice that amount or more. Scanning up and down at the crowds of people, Noah hoped to see an unruly mop of brown, curly hair. If she didn't come back soon, he would need to leave his post and spend money he hadn't earned yet on one of those sausages he could smell barbecuing somewhere over towards the car-park.

When he thought his stomach couldn't take any more of the mouth watering smell, his dad appeared from nowhere with three sausages in bread buried in onions and tomato sauce.

"You look busy — want a snag?" He handed him one without waiting for an answer. "Where's Mel? I got one for her, too; thought she might need some meat." Noah suddenly hoped she wasn't coming back anytime soon; his sausage didn't touch the sides.

"Can you do us a portrait please, Noah?" The familiar voice purred right behind him. He turned around quickly and looked straight into the glowing face of Laura Penrose once again. She had her arm firmly looped with the arm of a guy probably two years or so older and at least two feet taller.

"Um, yes, sure; take a seat," he shoved the last piece of sausage in and watched as his dad mouthed 'I'll go find Mel,' and left him to it.

It didn't seem to matter to Laura they had one seat between them. Noah turned around to find her perched happily on the lap of her moody looking boyfriend, who looked extremely bored by the whole thing.

"Do we have to sit long?" His voice sounded gruff, but quiet. Noah sighed as he reached into his bag for his small sketch pad.

"Give me a couple of minutes to do a rough sketch, then you can go and do what you want to do for ten minutes. I'll be done by then." The pencil in his hand hovered over the paper as he looked up at the pair to take in their features. He already knew Laura's face pretty well and probably could have sketched her without needing to look, but this guy she was with — he needed to take a mental photo so he could capture his likeness perfectly. He had a square jaw, full lips with the faintest Elvis curl, thick-set brow framed with dark brown eyebrows and eyes so blue he swore they were coloured contacts. He could also swear he had seen them before, in fact, all the pieces of this face seemed familiar to him.

Noah's hand trembled as he began to sketch, quick flicks with the pencil as his face bobbed up and down, his eyes shifting from paper to people.

"Okay, you're right to go now. I've got what I need. Come back in fifteen minutes and I'll have the finished picture for you." He didn't even look up as the pair climbed off the chair and left; Laura giggled and cooed, her friend silent.

Noah picked up his large sketch-pad and set to work. It took little time to transfer the picture from the smaller pad to the one he used especially for selling. And as he added the last few bits of shading here and there he couldn't take his eyes off the face of Laura's new boyfriend. He wiped his brow, surprised to realize he had been sweating.

"So, made oodles of money yet?" It was Mel. She looked a little hot and bothered.

"Only the one so far...take a look." He didn't look at her at first; he needed to see if she felt anything like he did when she saw the picture.

It didn't take long. She looked at the sketch, her brow crumpled like it always did when she concentrated; her mouth opened and closed several times before looking at Noah. "Who the hell is this? He looks kind of like... it can't be though..." She sat down opposite and scratched her head.

"I know. He looks like Sarah's sketch, but it's impossible. He's far too young...unless he's a frigging time traveller." Noah almost chocked on those last two words.

Fuck me. Ghosts! Special powers! Why the hell not time travellers too.

He felt irritated, something was niggling at him – a distant memory, a small detail, he had buried so long ago.

"There was something rather distinctive about Laura's boyfriend. His little finger on his right hand...or rather the lack of it. I've seen a hand with that missing finger somewhere before, Mel. I had the exact same feeling about that bloody tattoo. I don't know why, but I'm sure they're connected."

Noah grabbed Mel's arm and she swung around. His grip tightened as the pair of them couldn't take their eyes off the couple who were walking back to pick up their portrait.

Noah could see Mel's confusion. She was scared too. And he couldn't understand why he felt exactly the same.

Chapter Fourteen

The rest of the morning passed by in a blur; Noah had a few more customers and even managed to find his mum a present. But he couldn't wait to pack up and go home. He needed to see Sarah.

"I'm coming with you," Mel touched his arm in the car and her mind mirrored his own thoughts. He sometimes suspected she had 'the knowing' too.

They hardly spoke two words until they had both helped take the things from the car and were heading down to the beach.

"If you think there's a connection between the monster that was there the night Sarah died and this new boyfriend of Laura's, maybe Sarah knows something she's not telling." Mel spoke over her shoulder as she paced ahead of Noah down the steps. At first glance, the beach was deserted, but Noah's smile told her Sarah was there. She was always there.

"Well, hello strangers." Sarah looked distracted somehow; not her usual bubbly self.

"You okay?" Noah sat down next to her, a feeling of dread in his stomach.

She glanced out to sea, its grey moodiness matched in her eyes.

Noah took the sketch out of his bag and handed it to her

while waiting for her answer.

He said nothing — just watched her face as she studied the picture he'd given her.

"That's him! He's the one you need to look out for!" She looked up at Noah, her eyes wide until she realized what she had said and she lowered her gaze to the sand.

"What's going on, Sarah? So we're not looking for the same guy who killed you?"

Noah touched her arm firmly, desperately wanting to see what she was hiding.

"No, Noah, you're not. I can only tell you what has already happened, I can't pass on what I've seen in the future; but I know the two events are connected. I hoped with 'the knowing' you'd be able to figure out the rest. And it looks like you're on the right path, Noah. I'm so relieved it's beginning to unfold because I'm running out of time." She looked into his eyes, straight into his soul and he ached with a sadness he couldn't begin to measure.

"What's she saying, Noah?" Mel sounded annoyed and Noah realized he'd almost forgotten she was there. He filled her in, but he didn't take his eyes off Sarah.

Mel looked even more annoyed once he'd finished.

"...I don't get it. Who the hell are we meant to be looking for then?" It was a question Noah was about to ask.

"You've got to stop what's going to happen — what happened to me is over, nobody can change that now."

"So it's him? The guy from the market this morning; he's the one we're looking for? But you can't tell us what he's going to do, or who he's going to do it to? Surely it must be here, right, on this beach. Why would you be here if it wasn't?" Noah knew he was waffling — speaking his thoughts out loud. Something gnawed away at him. Sarah had said she was running out of time and he felt terrified to ask what she meant by that.

*****

"Well, at least we know who we're after now; that loser boyfriend of Laura's. She's in your sister's class isn't she? Maybe she knows a bit more about the new love of Laura's life."

They were heading back to Noah's place. Both of them had been lost in their own thoughts until now.

There were a million and one questions swimming around Noah's head; things seemed to fit, but didn't make sense. Like the tattoo. He wished Sarah could tell them more than she let on. He was also pissed with her for not helping them to help her. Why did it have to be all up to him, anyway? None of it made sense.

He rubbed his temple.

"Got a headache?" Mel inquired with concern.

Noah managed a smile.

"I'm fine." He lied. He didn't feel it. Not one bit.

*****

When they got back to Noah's, Kayla was standing in the front yard with her mobile pushed into her ear and a Cheshire cat grin on her face. She didn't even look up at them as they walked in through the open door.

Mel slumped onto the couch; she looked as moody as Noah felt.

"Want a drink?" Noah walked to the fridge and grabbed two cans of coke but put one back when he saw her shake her head.

"So, all we have to do now is work out what he's going to

79

do, who he's going to do it to, and where he's going to do it."
Mel grabbed a cushion and hugged it to her chest like it had
only now dawned on her they were still a million miles away
from solving this mystery.

Noah knew exactly what she meant though — just like
putting a jigsaw puzzle together when you didn't have all the
pieces or the picture on the box.

"We've got to find out more about our man. I think you
should have a little chat with Miss big boobs." Mel looked
away from him when she said the last part.

Noah could feel his face turning scarlet. Was that what was
getting to her? He assumed it was the mystery they were
working on.

"Why do I have to talk to her?" He felt terrified by the idea,
but tried not to show it.

Mel sighed, "She wouldn't even look at me, let alone talk to
me; I'm completely the wrong sex."

Noah's laugh turned to relief when Mel joined in, her eyes
sparkling once more.

At that moment Kayla breezed in, her face positively
glowing as she hummed a tune to herself.

"What's made you so happy?" He called to her as she
floated down the hallway.

"Not what... who!" She called back.

"Have you got a minute?" Now was as good a time as any
to ask her about Laura; he stole a quick glance at Mel who
nodded at him encouragingly.

She sauntered back into the room still grinning.

"What d'you want, Noahie?" God, she *was* in a good
mood. She hadn't called him that for years.

"I did a sketch for Laura Penrose and her boyfriend this morning. I wondered if she'd spoken about him at all."

Kayla folded herself into the armchair opposite him and suddenly looked extremely smug.

"Well, all I can say is she'd better hold onto that sketch because she's not going to be holding onto him for much longer."

Noah glanced at Mel who looked as puzzled as he must have looked.

"You wouldn't know much about him, would you?"

"I might. Why are you interested?" She looked suspicious suddenly as she started to stand up. Noah was afraid her happy mood had dissolved and she wouldn't want to answer any more of his silly questions.

"Oh, it's just that his face is really familiar and well, if I had a name maybe I could remember where I know him from..."

"His name's Jackson," her eyes had glazed over suddenly as she made herself comfortable again. "Jackson Sylvester."

"...Sylvester?" Noah glanced at Mel again. Her mouth gaped like a floundering fish.

"Yes, if you must know — he's Mr. S's nephew."

It was definitely one of those face palm moments. So that was the connection. And why he'd looked so familiar to them; he was clearly the spitting image of his father.

"So...Mr. S's nephew? Does his family live down here then?" This was brilliant, and more information than the three of them had managed to find out in the last two weeks.

"Umm, well he moved down here a month ago with his

mum; he finished school last year and has been accepted at Franklyn University..." she stopped mid sentence as her mobile rang. Noah jumped. Kayla shot out of the chair and squeezed her hand into her jeans pocket to pull out the tiny phone and sauntered back out the door into the front yard again.

Chapter Fifteen

"What the...?" Mel, as always, mirrored Noah's own thoughts. "Do you think...?"

It suddenly hit Noah with the force of a cricket ball in the nose. Yes, he did think. And he didn't like it one little bit.

Mel stumbled to express the thoughts in her head. "Is he...with her? ...but that means...! Oh my God! It's father and son isn't it! If the father was responsible for Sarah's death, then just what the hell is his son capable of?" She leapt off the couch and pressed her hands to her mouth — her eyes wide with fear.

Noah suddenly felt sick. It all began to make sense. But Sarah showed more concern for this boy and needing them to stop him doing something really bad. The pieces were coming together and the picture did not look good. He could even understand why Sarah had picked him to help her. It was beginning to look like his sister might well be in great danger.

Noah's mobile chimed to announce a new message. It was Nick. He wanted to know if he could call around — he had some news for them.

So much had happened and neither of them had given a thought to fill Nick in on it all. Noah's stomach did a guilty flip as he texted back to say Nick could call around anytime.

And in less than a minute Nick's perfectly sculptured head

of hair poked around the side of the front door, "Anyone home?" He grinned.

Bouncing in without an invitation, Nick threw himself onto the couch in the middle of his two friends; and looking smug with himself, turned to Noah and said, "I think I've found who we're looking for." His deep, brown eyes flicked from Noah to Mel, then back again. Noah could hear Kayla coming back inside so he pushed his finger onto his lips and shook his head at Nick; who appeared puzzled, but soon got the message.

She almost skipped back up the hallway; everything about her radiated something Noah had never seen in her before. He heard her bedroom door close and he gulped.

"What's going on? I've found our man. Don't you two want to know who I think it is?" He must have been itching to share his knowledge.

Noah didn't want to rain on his parade so he glanced at Mel and raising an eyebrow, turned to Nick and said, "Go on then, fill us in on the news."

Nick pulled his phone out from his pocket, pushing on the screen as he passed it to Noah to show him the picture he'd taken barely half an hour before. It was Jackson Sylvester.

Noah nodded and passed it to Mel who silently handed it back to Nick who sighed deeply.

"When did you two find out?" Noah couldn't help laugh at how dejected Nick looked. Mel smacked Nick's arm in a 'there, there' gesture and proceeded to fill him in on the sketch at the market of him and Laura, their last meeting with Sarah and lastly, the conversation they'd had with Kayla.

"Holy shit!" As always, Nick had a way of summing things up rather well. "Do you think Kayla's involved?" Noah thought the world of him, but Nick wasn't the sharpest tool in the shed.

"What are we going to do? You have got to tell her she can't see him — tell her he's bad," added Nick. He seemed as scared for Kayla as Noah felt; he had always had a soft spot for her.

"Like that'd make any difference. You know what she's like; you can't tell her anything once she's made her mind up, and besides, I haven't seen her this happy since – well never." Noah dropped his face into his hands; it would seem that's exactly where Kayla's safety was right now, too.

"I'm going to have to use the knowing, we have to keep track of her every movement." He glanced up again and rubbed his temples — his head was throbbing and so were his gums.

"We need to learn more about him too – where he lives, where he goes, and more than anything, where the hell his dad is. Surely we can find a way to make the guy responsible for Sarah's death finally pay for what he did?" Nick fiddled with his phone nervously.

"Where did you get that photo of him?" It was the first thing Mel had said since Nick arrived.

Nick flushed bright scarlet and shifted uncomfortably in his seat. "I was umm, at the park for a late lunch, you know, just finished helping dad out and thought I'd sit on the bench and, you know, watch the world go by..." he looked like he was hiding a mortal sin.

"You were checking out guys!!" Mel threw her cushion at him and giggled.

Nick laughed too, his embarrassment fading as Noah joined in as well.

"You've got to admit, he's pretty hot. He did catch my eye, but only because he looked so God-damn happy talking to someone on his mobile. But before you go thinking I've been secretly taking pictures of every attractive guy in the neighbourhood — well I haven't. I took it because he looked so much like that photo in the school yearbook we saw of Mr. S's brother – I put two and two together and well..." he petered off as Noah's mum walked out of her office to make herself a snack, and for a while at least, the three of them couldn't say any more. She made them all something to eat as well, not Kayla though; she didn't want food, which made Noah even more concerned — she never said no to food.

While they were eating, Noah's mum offered to go with them to the Plaza as she had some errands to run. Mel jumped at the chance, "Yeah sure, why not, some retail therapy would be good right now." Noah didn't mind the distraction either and he needed the driving practice, but he felt anxious about leaving Kayla home alone; a thought that wouldn't have crossed his mind yesterday. But now things were different.

"Maybe Kayla would like to come along, too," Noah jumped up and went to ask hoping she would; at least it would stop him worrying for a while if she did.

*****

"Should we follow her?" Nick showed concern for Kayla too as the three of them watched her stroll off towards the nearest clothes boutique. They'd all agreed to meet up with Noah's mum at the food court in two hours.

"No, she'll get suspicious, and cranky. I kind of like her this happy, I hope it's not me who has to burst her bubble." He thought about how upset she had been about her last boyfriend. Noah didn't like the idea of having to break his own sister's heart when she was clearly smitten with this guy.

Mel grinned at the pair of them, "Okay then guys. Who's got money?" Spoken like a true woman. She linked each of their arms and led them towards her favourite accessory shop. There was no hiding her inner thoughts and feelings from

Noah though, as he caught the flash and saw the turmoil festering in her mind.

"Well I've just got paid and I'm feeling a little generous so you might be in luck," said Nick, tapping his back pocket. But Nick's thoughts weren't any less confused, either. Noah had a horrible feeling Nick had fallen under Jackson's spell, too. He also harboured great concern for Kayla's safety. For a moment Noah's stomach felt hollow; he had no idea how they were going to solve this without anyone getting hurt.

*****

"It's about time!" Kayla was sitting at one of the small tables, her legs crossed and her hands hugging a large, foaming cup of hot chocolate. She didn't sound at all upset. "Have you seen Mum?"

Noah and Nick pulled up two chairs from the empty table next to them and sat down.

"I'll have what she's having — can I get anyone else anything?" Mel grabbed her purse from her bag and getting no response from Noah or Nick, went to get herself a drink.

"No, haven't seen her at all...you been waiting long?" Noah studied her face desperate to see her thoughts. She seemed different somehow, like she'd grown up overnight.

"Half an hour, but that's okay. I spent up in the first shop." She smirked sheepishly, "I was hoping to scab some more cash off Mum!"

"Yeah? Good luck with that. You know Mum's as tight as a duck's arse!" interjected Noah.

Kayla laughed, which was a mistake because she had a mouthful of hot chocolate at the time and ended up spraying most of it all over Nick who, for one brief moment, looked completely horrified. Noah folded himself in half with laughter. Kayla tried desperately to stop, but only made things worse, "Oh Noahie, that's your bloody fault!" She smacked him playfully on the arm and suddenly Noah's whole world filled with Jackson Sylvester – his face, his gentle hands, his soft gruff voice; and the kind, sweet words he uttered to Kayla. Noah reeled in complete repulsion and shut his eyes, desperate to block out the images. Anger rose inside from the pit of his stomach and reached up to his throat into a livid cry, which he desperately wanted to release. *How could this bastard be so damn charming to Kayla when he could be capable of doing who knew what?*

"You okay?" Mel sat down with her hot chocolate and hadn't missed that look on his face.

"Just a pain in the head, that's all." Noah brushed it off; he didn't want to spoil the moment. Kayla hadn't seen the look, she was still giggling with Nick and the four of them continued to laugh and crack jokes until Noah's mum turned up.

Chapter Sixteen

Noah stood on the beach. It was quiet; empty just the way he liked it. The sea was flat, calm, the perfect slack tide. He watched intently as two seagulls circled overhead in the cloudless sky. One of the seagulls cried out — a shrill, piercing sound that morphed into the scream of a girl. He reeled around and saw Kayla. She was farther up the beach towards the cave but she wasn't alone. He was with her. Jackson Sylvester. He was talking quickly, his mouth moving but the words were silent to Noah's ears. Kayla cried out again, a piercing, heartbreaking scream that ripped through to his heart. And then, with a speed and force Noah couldn't comprehend, Jackson grabbed her hair and dragged her like an unloved rag-doll, into the cave where the two of them seemed to disappear into a tunnel of blackness. Noah cried out but no sound would come; he tried to run after them but his legs wouldn't move. He retched with the pain and frustration of feeling helpless and closed his eyes to blink away the tears. He opened them again and was in his room. It was only a dream; it wasn't real. The tears were, though. His face was drenched as he wiped it with his hand, but the tears wouldn't stop.

*****

Noah kicked the bed sheets off; the singlet he wore had glued to his chest with sweat. His head pounded and he felt seriously sick. Twisting his legs around to the side of the bed, he sat upright and waited out the bout of nausea. A slither of light lit up under his door and he could hear the murmurings of someone talking. Glancing at his digital clock he saw it was only just after 4am. Who was up?Curiosity outweighed the feeling of throwing up and he opened his door to see. Both the light and the whispered talking were coming from Kayla's room for one fearful moment Noah thought she had company. He pushed his ear into the door — desperate to make out what was being said and could immediately tell she was talking on her phone. Noah sighed with relief as his fight or flight instincts stood down.

"...I know what you're saying Jack, but she really thinks you're her boyfriend. Shit! It drives me mental hearing her talking about you to all her smarmy friends." There was a pause; Kayla laughed, "You're going to have to keep telling her 'til she gets the message...or shall I?" Another pause — Noah could hardly breathe; there was her laugh again. "Well, that's charming! I love you, too! Okay then, if you think it'll work...when?" She said nothing for a while, then "Great! See you then. Can't wait to see you..." her voice was a whisper and Noah strained his ears, but all he could hear was the sound of his own beating heart. He turned around, and sloped back to bed where he lay awake until morning.

Chapter Seventeen

"You've got to find out where and when they're meeting Noah; she can't be left alone with this guy." Mel punctuated the last word with a yawn — it was only 6am and Noah hadn't been able to wait any longer to let her know what he'd heard earlier that morning. Her voice husky from sleep, he thought she sounded strangely cute.

"I know, Mel. Don't worry, I'll find out. Sorry to ruin your Sunday morning lie-in but I really needed to talk to you." He hadn't meant for it to come out like that; he felt his heart thumping and he swore he could hear Mel smiling.

"...it's okay. I didn't sleep very well, either. Will you let me know as soon as you know what she's doing, so I can come with you?"

He was glad of that. Nick would be working with his dad again today, so he couldn't be around. That wasn't much of a disappointment; he liked the excuse of being alone with Mel.

"Yeah, I will. Thanks Mel. I'll call you later." He lay back on his bed and closed his eyes, just for a moment. Before he knew it, he had drifted off to sleep.

Noah opened his eyes and stretched sleepily. Glancing over at the clock on his bedside table he swiftly shot out of bed in a panic; it was almost 11 o'clock. His heart lurched and he suddenly felt sick in the pit of his stomach. What if he'd missed Kayla?

He swore to himself as he scrambled to put on his jeans and a T-shirt. *Oh God, please let her still be home.*

When he opened the door he could make out voices in the kitchen – three voices. His eyes rolled skyward as he heard Kayla's voice and laughter — she sounded uncharacteristically bright and cheerful again. The other voice was Mum, she was laughing too. But the third voice...it wasn't his dad; he would be at the garage this morning. He cocked his head to listen and then dread overwhelmed him instantly — it had to be *him.*

Running a shaky hand through his hair, Noah straightened his back and strolled into the kitchen trying to look more casual than he felt.

"Good morning, sleepy head!" Mum was making tea and Kayla and Jackson were both seated on the stools at the kitchen bench, their eyes locked onto each other while Jackson spoke.

"Hey," Noah mumbled, sounding half asleep — he didn't feel it. He walked around the bench and gave his mum a hug and a kiss on the cheek. "Happy birthday, Mum," A huge bouquet of flowers were crammed into his mum's favourite vase next to the microwave. Noah hoped they were from his dad and not this smarmy sleaze bag sitting next to his sister.

Kayla turned around and beamed at him while jumping off the stool. "Hi Noah, this is Jackson — Jackson this is my brother, Noah," she looked from one to the other still grinning. Noah couldn't speak for what felt like an eternity, but then this young man he was looking at; this person he feared more than he'd feared anyone in his life did something that completely took him by surprise; he held out his hand and smiled.

"Kayla didn't tell me you were such a talented artist," said Jackson.

For the briefest of moments, Noah considered shaking the offered hand, but his eyes were drawn to the stump where the little finger should have been and that anger returned to the pit of his stomach. He mentally shook his head instead.

"So, your uncle teaches us Biology, is your dad as cool as his brother?" asked Noah.

Jackson's eyes lowered as he mumbled something about his dad not being around any more. Kayla glared at her brother with a threatening look. Noah quickly changed the subject.

"How's Laura?" he asked. Kayla's face twitched for a split second and then she laughed.

Jackson joined in before replying, "It's a long story."

I've got all day, thought Noah.

Jackson continued, "Her mum used to baby-sit me apparently, and when I moved down here two months ago Laura offered to show me around. I didn't really mind to begin with, but she's been telling everyone I'm her boyfriend and she's the kind of girl who likes to get what she wants, if you know what I mean."

Yes, Noah had a pretty good idea. I think your dad suffered from the same affliction.

"What about getting that sketch done of the two of you?" Noah inquired. It was a fair question.

"Like I say," Jackson replied, smiling. "She doesn't like to take no for an answer. That's why I wasn't very sociable. I only agreed to do it because I thought she'd let me off the hook once I had."

Kayla placed her hand on Jackson's shoulder and turning to Noah, she said, "It's okay, though. We've got a plan that will give her the message once and for all."

Kayla sounded strangely devious and Noah's hair prickled on the back of his neck. A gnawing feeling grew in the back of his mind, as something began to dawn on him. Maybe it wasn't Kayla who was in danger – what if it was Laura? And the worst thing was maybe Kayla was going to be Jackson's willing partner in crime.

*****

"You've got to be shitting me!" Mel sounded as freaked out as Noah had been when the thought first hit him.

"I know. You should've seen the two of them and the look in Kayla's eyes when she said about having a plan that would give Laura the message once and for all." Noah bit his nails, something he hadn't done for a long time.

"Do you think we need to warn Laura?" She didn't wait for his reply. "I'm coming over. We've got to think this through – see you in a bit," and she was gone.

Noah was back in his room. He didn't want to be around those two at the moment; their obvious affection for each other made him want to puke. He thought about how upset Kayla had been about the last jerk she'd gone out with, and how he'd tried to get her to do something she didn't want to do. Was love so blind that she'd do something so terrible this time?

There was an angry knock on his door. Before replying, his sister stormed in. "Why did you have to ask him about his dad?" She looked furious.

"I was just making conversation," Noah was taken back by her obvious concern for this guy she'd only known for a short time.

Her voice dropped to a whisper. "His dad died in a motorbike accident when Jackson was only 8. Shit, Noah! His dad was only 26. He doesn't like to talk about it, so don't mention it again, okay?" She walked out without waiting for a reply.

Mel arrived within ten minutes; she'd scored a lift from her mum. Noah was grateful she hadn't made him wait any longer to see her.

She breezed into Noah's room with a smile and a cloud of that perfume she always wore. She smelled like the jasmine growing along the back fence; heady and intoxicating.

"Hey knucklehead; well don't they make a cute and cosy couple?" Mel pulled a face from seeing Kayla and Jackson lounging on the couch together watching a movie.

"Why do you think I'm in here?" replied Noah. He moved a pile of books from his computer chair but Mel threw herself onto the bed next to where he had been sitting and kicked off her shoes. He filled her in on the conversation he'd had with Kayla just before.

"Well, I guess that draws a line under Rocky's part of the story," said Mel, thoughtfully, "My mum would call that Karma."

Noah had a feeling Sarah already knew that was the case.

"So, when are they going to see Laura?" asked Mel. Noah stared at her painted toe nails — each one bright blue with a perfectly painted black smiley face. He smirked. "Well, Kayla will see her at school tomorrow, but they're definitely plotting something to do together. Maybe we should go see Sarah again and keep her informed." Noah answered as he parked himself at the end of his bed.

Mel didn't look like she wanted to go anywhere. "Yeah, I guess so. But we don't really know much yet. You need to find out when this is all going down and we can make a plan to be there to stop it."

"You could go and ask!" Noah ducked as he spoke, but not quickly enough. Mel landed one on his left arm.

"Okay, bruiser, I'll go get you a drink and no, I'm sorry but we don't have any chocolate in the house," he said, smirking. She couldn't hide anything from him.

"You're a freak!" Mel chuckled as he left to grab a cold drink for her from the fridge.

Kayla and Jackson were whispering to each other when he walked out. He wished Sarah had given him bionic ears as well as the knowing.

"Hey Noahie, can you grab us a couple of cans, too, please?" He couldn't believe how nice Kayla was being with him — he could get used to it.

Noah leaned over the couch and handed them each a can. Kayla squeezed his arm in the spot Mel had punched, but he felt no pain.

"Well, it's set for Tuesday about 5 o'clock at the back beach." Noah announced as he walked back into his room.

"Jeez, it doesn't give us much time. We'd better go see Sarah then, and let her know." Mel took a deep swig of the fizzy drink, burped, put it down on the bedside table and put her shoes back on. Noah grabbed his denim jacket from the back of his computer chair; he figured now would be as good a time as any.

Chapter Eighteen

Noah's mobile rang as he closed the front door behind him.

"Hey!" It was Nick. "Are you doing anything this afternoon?" His dad didn't need him for the rest of the day and he sounded at a loose end.

"We're on our way to see Sarah. It's all going down Tuesday, Nick." Noah held the phone between himself and Mel so she could hear as Nick swore loudly, and they both laughed.

"I'll see you both at the beach — don't leave until I get there."

"Well, I guess it'll be the three amigos for Tuesday then." Mel linked her arm through Noah's and they walked silently the rest of the way.

He could feel Mel's warmth, it felt nice. She was as unsure about it all as Noah. He could see how muddled she felt about the whole thing. She also hadn't got a clue how they were going to stop someone from getting hurt or worse. There was concern about Laura's safety, even though Noah could see how much she didn't like her. It suddenly struck Noah how lucky he felt to be going through all of this with Mel. He couldn't have done it without her.

Noah felt sick at the thought of what his own sister might be about to do, or at least try to do. He couldn't get the picture out of his mind of her and Jackson — cuddled up together on the couch, partners in crime and so damn happy about it, too. There were still so many things that didn't make sense.

There were a few people on the beach. 'Fair weather friends' his mum called them; those who were always more willing to exercise when the sun shone.

Sarah waved at them as they hopped down the bottom few steps onto the beach.

"It's all happening on Tuesday," Noah sat down next to Sarah and wondered how many more times he'd be able to do this, "and Rocky died probably not that long after you – in a motorbike accident."

She smiled at him — one of her knowing smiles. He was certain she had known that all along.

"We think it has to be Laura who's in danger, not Kayla as we first suspected. But I think Kayla might be a part of it, too. They seem to have a plan to get rid of her, but I don't know — maybe it's all going to go wrong. It still doesn't feel right though, Sarah. You should see the two of them together, I've never seen her so damn happy." Noah ran his hand through his hair.

"You'll be fine, Noah," she said.

He wished he could feel as confident about himself as Sarah did.

"I don't know how to deal with this, though. Do we confront them here at the beach or would it be best to hide somewhere and wait for the moment something is about to happen? What if we do that and we're too late?" Noah's head pulsed and his chest hurt. He'd never felt so stressed about anything before now.

"You can't talk to them before; I think the cave would be the perfect place to watch everything unfold. I'll be here too

Noah — I can stay close to them and not be seen."

How the hell can Sarah look so serene about it all? "Well, why can't you stop it all happening? Why do you need me?" Anger welled up in Noah again. Sarah had this way of being able to bring out a whole myriad of emotions in him at the drop of a hat.

"I can't interfere like that, Noah. I can only use you — that's the rule." Noah had always hated rules.

Mel touched his arm and grounded him instantly. He turned to her and smiled lopsidedly.

"Well, it looks like we're on our own, Mel." She already knew anyway. Except they weren't; Nick was striding up the beach towards them.

"Hey!" He threw himself on the sand instinctively leaving the space where Sarah sat. "Okay, fill me in."

Chapter Nineteen

Noah walked onto the train and parked himself in the first empty seat closest to the door. He dropped his backpack onto the seat beside him and pulled a piece of paper from the side pocket.

Written on it was the address Sarah had given him that morning. He studied the curly writing, tracing it with his finger.

This was something he had to do. It'd been bothering him for too long now and Sarah was running out of time. It would all be coming to a head tomorrow whatever the hell that meant. This had to be done today. He'd wagged school enough times in the past to know the drill. He left the house at the right time this morning but instead of heading to school he went straight to the beach to see Sarah. She didn't even seem surprised to see him and it hadn't taken him long to explain what he wanted to do. She'd sat silently while he spoke and nodded her head as she cried. But she didn't argue with him or even try to stop him. She wrote down the address for him and had simply said two words to him as he got up to leave:

"Thank you."

He watched out of the window as the scenery changed from trees and hills to concrete and sprawling suburbs. The sound of the wheels on the tracks was hypnotic, Noah rocked gently from the speed of the express train – he wanted to close his eyes for a moment, but he couldn't afford to fall asleep. Time wasn't on his side and he had to get this right today.

After what felt like an eternity, Noah sighed as he heard the electronic voice announce the next station — his stop.

His stomach gurgled and he had an overwhelming need to go to the toilet, he hated how that happened when he got nervous. He could only think about Sarah, and how important this would be for her.

He stood on the platform and took a look around to try to get his bearings. It didn't take him long to work out which direction he needed to go once he'd checked maps on his mobile. Mel had told him the address was within an easy walk from the station.

The tree lined street had an air of serenity. Golden leaves crunched under his feet as he checked for numbers on letter boxes to find the right house.

96. The shiny brass number was on the wooden gate. He pushed it open and walked up the narrow path to the frosted glass front door. His finger poised above the doorbell and for a moment, a split second, he thought about running, but a shadowy figure moved towards the door and he realized it was too late. Noah felt like a child who had been caught out about to perform 'knock door run'. The door opened slowly and he found himself staring into Sarah's eyes — only these were the eyes of a soul filled with sadness and loss.

"Mrs. Nicholson?" He didn't need to ask. Of course it was Sarah's mum.

"You aren't selling anything, are you? I'm sorry, but we're not interested." She started to close the door again without even waiting for an answer. Noah stuck his foot out and looked at her with what he hoped would be a persuasive smile.

"No, I'm here about Sarah."

"You're not a policeman or from the press — what is this about?" Her eyes narrowed with suspicion.

"I'm a friend, a friend of Sarah's."

Her eyes flickered from suspicion to utter confusion, but she opened the door for him and he followed her into a comfortable sitting room. There were two leather couches opposite each other separated by a chunky wooden coffee table. A huge open fireplace dominated the room with its dark wooden mantle piece. All along the top were framed photos of Sarah at different ages of her short life.

"How can you be a friend of Sarah's? You don't look any older than she was..." she petered off and crossed her arms in front of her, defensively.

"Mrs. Nicholson, is your husband here?"

She shook her head. "No, he's at the shop this morning but he'll be back soon." She glanced at a gold watch on her tiny wrist.

"My name's Noah, Noah Cooper. I live by Ryde back beach and three weeks ago I had an accident there."

He watched her mouth twitch in the corner as he mentioned the place Sarah had been killed. She sat down opposite him silently as Noah opened his backpack and pulled out his sketchpad.

"I've seen your daughter — she came to me after the accident." He placed the sketchpad onto the table and turned it around for her to see. She picked it up with trembling hands, and tears flooded from her eyes when she saw his sketch.

"I don't understand. My daughter's..." she started to sob then and Noah shifted in his seat awkwardly. He wondered whether he should comfort her.

He continued. He told her everything except about the gift — he didn't want to completely freak this poor woman out.

And when he got to the part about Mel seeing Sarah write the note on his sketchpad he flicked the page over for her to see what Sarah had written to her that day on the beach.

Mrs. Nicholson's mouth fell open as she read the words.

"This is Sarah's writing; but how can she..?" She looked up at Noah, her eyes wide with something he hadn't seen in them when she first answered the door.

Noah carried on talking — it all came flooding out like he had no choice in the matter. He told her everything; what Sarah had said about dying; how happy she looked, but he also told her exactly what had happened that night and how she had died in that cave.

Noah glanced around the room and spotted a box of tissues on the window ledge. He reached over for them and placed them gently on the table.

"Can I get you a glass of water?" He asked as he stood next to the weeping woman, his hand hovered over her shoulder awkwardly as he helplessly watched this poor mother who'd lost her child far too young, so long ago. She nodded.

He found the kitchen; it was filled with the delicious smell of a freshly baked fruit cake cooling on the bench. Nothing left in the sink and no piles of mail or magazines on the surface — he'd never seen such a tidy kitchen. Opening the cupboards Noah found a glass without too much trouble, filled it from the tap, walked back to the sitting room and handed it to the lady as she finished blowing her nose.

"I knew it hadn't been an accident. Sarah would not have been there alone. The police weren't interested in pursuing it. They found no evidence of foul play, but we knew she'd been murdered." She took a few sips before putting the glass down with a shaky hand.

Noah picked up the sketchpad and turned the pages to the

sketch of Robert Sylvester. He handed it to her.

"He died soon after all this happened. He was killed in a motorbike accident. He left behind a son, he was only 8. And it's him that we're watching out for now. Sarah said there's going to be another murder on this beach unless we stop it and that's why she came back."

Noah expected to see anger in her eyes as she studied the face of her daughter's killer, but there was no rage — only sorrow. She sighed as she put the pad back onto the table and then, for the first time since being there, the woman in front of him smiled.

"That sounds like our Sarah. So she's asked you to help? And you've found all of this information out yourself, Noah?"

He nodded. He told her how they'd finally found the connection between the man who had killed her and his son, and what was going to happen if they didn't stop it.

"You'd make a great detective. Did she send you here?" She took some more of the water as she waited for him to answer.

"No, it was my idea, but she gave me something to give you when I told her I would be coming to see you this morning." He reached into his backpack again and pulled out a folded piece of paper. He handed it to this woman he had only met, but felt like he had known forever and watched as she brought the note to her face. She closed her eyes and smelt it. She stroked it tenderly as though she could touch her daughter once more through this simple piece of paper her daughter had touched herself.

"I think perhaps we'd better have a cup of tea before I read this, don't you?" She stood up then and with lightness to her step she walked out into the kitchen.

Noah palmed his eyes and massaged his temples. He

couldn't believe it had been easier than he thought it would be.

She breezed back into the room with a plate loaded up with biscuits — the kind his mum never bought because they cost so much and never lasted more than one sitting.

"Help yourself Noah, by the way; please call me 'Trudy'." She smiled at him and he was struck once more by how much she looked like Sarah. "Oh, here comes Martin, he can smell tea leaves brewing in the pot from a mile away can that man!"

Noah jumped as he heard the front door open and close. His mouth dried up instantly and he remembered how much he had needed the toilet when he'd gotten off the train.

Mr. Nicholson walked into the room and did a double take when he saw Noah sitting there. Noah stood up to introduce himself, he held out his hand to the intimidating man who glared at him like he was something he'd just put his foot in.

"Hello Mr. Nicholson, my name's…"

"Who the hell are you? And what the bloody hell are you doing in my house?"

Noah glanced towards the kitchen and wondered where Trudy had gone; he silently prayed she'd be coming back sometime real soon.

"I'm Noah Cooper." Noah dropped his hand as it didn't look like the tall, broad shouldered man in front of him was likely to shake it.

"And what in the name of God are you doing in my house?" His voice boomed.

Noah tried to swallow and opened his mouth but had no idea what to say, where to begin.

"It's okay, Martin, this young lad knows our Sarah." Trudy walked back into the room with a tray filled with teacups, saucers, milk jug, sugar bowl and teapot.

Noah nearly laughed out loud as he stole a glance at the fuming Mr. Nicholson – this was starting to feel like some bizarre mad-hatter's tea party.

"He's been talking to our daughter, Martin." Trudy busied herself pouring the tea 'playing mum' so to speak, when her husband directed his anger onto her.

"What the hell are you doing letting crackpots like him into our home?" He stood up then, outraged at both her and Noah, and managed to knock the table with his leg causing a tea tsunami over the top of the three cups.

"I'd better go," Noah stood up — this was all too much and he didn't like the idea of hanging around any longer, but Trudy caught his arm and gently steered him to sit back down.

"This boy is not a crackpot, Martin — you've got to hear what he's told me and you'd believe it too."

Martin was still standing with his hands on his hips, which made him look even bigger than he had when he first walked into the room. Noah couldn't look at him. He hadn't seen any sign of the friendly, loving smile he had been wearing in the photo from the newspaper.

"So he can fill my head with absolute rubbish like he's done to you? You stupid woman, he's picked up this information and he's probably thinking of trying to do away with us so he can pinch anything worth stealing here."

"Oh for God's sake," Trudy's voice was barely audible at first and then, "SHUT UP AND SIT DOWN!" That part could have been heard all up and down the street. It worked though. Martin sat down but continued to glare at Noah like he'd have him in a headlock if he dared to make a move.

Trudy reached into the pocket of her skirt and passed her husband the note Sarah had written for them both.

Noah watched in silence, but he couldn't stop fidgeting.

Trudy passed him a cup of tea and told him to help himself to milk and sugar. He found himself unable to speak so he simply smiled at her. Noah's head was fit to burst. He'd seen the flash when Trudy touched his arm and the images had come thick and fast. He could see the pain she had gone through since losing Sarah, the bedroom left as a shrine, all the memories of her beautiful little girl and the love — so much love. He could also see the concern Trudy felt about her husband; he had heart problems — nothing major as yet, but it didn't stop her worrying about him. She wanted more than anything for him to sell the business. She'd always wanted to travel around Australia, but was afraid to ask him to give up the business he had put his life and soul into since their daughter's death. It was all too much to think about right now.

Noah's eyes shifted quickly back to Trudy's husband, who had pulled a pair of glasses from out of his jacket pocket, slowly he put them on and unfolded the note. Noah watched him as he surveyed the writing. Noah really had no idea what she had written on the note. He couldn't bring himself to read it even though he had thought about it while on the train.

Mr. Nicholson peered from under his glasses — his face softened and his eyes glazed. He looked from his wife to Noah and back again.

"I don't understand," he said, his voice suddenly small.

"How could this be...?" He stuck a finger under his glasses and wiped his eye as his wife shifted along the couch to be near to him; she placed her hand on his knee and leaned in to see the note for the first time herself.

Chapter Twenty

Noah glanced at his watch — it was getting on for three o'clock.

"I'm sorry Trudy and Martin, but I'd better think of heading off." He placed the photo album he'd been looking through onto the coffee table and sighed. He was comfortable and stuffed after a lovely lunch, endless pieces of cake and cups of tea; he'd have been happy to stay the night.

The three of them had spoken for hours. Trudy had helped to explain everything Noah had told her as Martin asked a million and one questions. There had been many tears along the way (some of them Noah's) and he had at last, got to see the side of Sarah's dad he had seen in the newspaper clipping. *Her folks were nice, really nice.*

They'd gone through the ringer eleven years ago after losing their only child. As Trudy had said, "No parent should outlive their child." Noah felt an empathy with them that took him by surprise.

He also felt a bond with them that made him feel guilty thinking of his own parents; he hadn't told them a thing about any of this.

"Could we drop you back?" Trudy asked him as she took Martin's hand and squeezed it.

"I want to go there with you, Noah. I have to see where it

all happened and perhaps…" she left the question unasked, but Noah knew exactly what she was thinking.

"I think Sarah would love to see you again, but I don't want you to be disappointed — you won't be able to see her as I do," Noah started to pile the cups and plates onto the tray and took them into the kitchen. He put the tray onto the bench and could hear the quiet talking filtering through from the sitting room.

For the first time all day his thoughts turned to tomorrow and he shivered with instant dread.

He wondered if Mel had missed him at school today; he also worried he'd be up shit creek by the time he got home. His phone vibrated in his jeans pocket and he pulled it out to check who had messaged him. Mel. It simply said:

Where r u? U OK?

He replied, telling her where he was and that he would be heading to the beach with the Nicholsons soon. She texted him back straight away:

WTF? Fone me wen u home xxx

He laughed to himself as he headed back into the sitting room — the talking had stopped. Trudy and Martin both stood up.

"Is it alright with you that we go now, or is there somewhere you need to be? We certainly don't want to get you into trouble or anything," Trudy said with concern as Noah laughed.

"Don't worry about that — it'll be great not to have to catch the train home, anyway."

It was more than great.

Martin's car was not what Noah expected — not at all. It was a beautifully kept 1970's Holden HQ Monaro; bronze with

109

white racing stripes on the boot and bonnet and the fish gills in the front fenders. Noah whistled as he walked all around the beast, nodding with admiration as he thought about how much his dad would have loved it, too. Sitting in the back Noah grinned when the middle aged man turned the key and the V8 fired into life. He could see Martin's eyes in the rear vision mirror and watched them come to life, too. Cars can do that to a man.

Noah closed his eyes and pushed back into the black, vinyl seat leaving the couple in the front seats to their own thoughts. He had more than enough of his own to work through.

They made a quick stop on the way, Trudy wanted to buy some flowers for Sarah – Tiger-lilies — they had always been her favourite. Noah watched her walk back to the car with the huge bouquet as it suddenly dawned on him how crazy this all was, how amazing these people who hadn't known him from Adam that morning, had put their faith in him after years of having very little.

The V8 gurgled to a halt into the empty beach car park. Noah hoped the beach would be empty, too. He jumped out of the car and asked Martin more about it while the two of them waited for Trudy. She nervously fixed her hair with a comb and a small compact from her bag. Martin opened the door for her; he obviously didn't want to linger any longer. Noah felt a little awkward as he led the way to the familiar wooden steps.

"We haven't been here...well, since it happened."

Noah wouldn't turn around to look at the woman; he didn't want to see the tears he could hear in her voice. He could only think about Sarah now and he spotted her half way down the steps and waved. Thankfully, the only other visitors to the beach were seagulls.

"She's here?" Martin's voice was barely audible over the crashing waves. Noah nodded unable to talk — there was a huge lump in his throat as he watched Sarah cup her mouth and nose with her two hands.

The next few moments were utterly surreal.

Martin had his arm around Trudy's shoulders; it was difficult to tell who was holding who up.

"Noah, I want you to ask Sarah something for me." Martin's cheeks were wet with tears and his eyes were wide with the wonder of it all. Noah nodded; he'd been waiting for this — a test.

"She can hear you," said Noah.

"Sarah, could you tell Noah what you made me for Father's Day when you were ten years old and where I keep it?"

Noah looked at Sarah, waiting for her to answer. She started to giggle, which was infectious and Noah laughed too, when she told him the answer.

"She made you a hideous ashtray at school and painted it black, white and red — your footy team colours. And even though it was the ugliest thing anyone had ever given you, you kept it on your bedside table and would put your loose change into it every night before going to bed because you don't smoke and just because Sarah made it especially for you." Noah smiled as Martin and Trudy laughed through their tears.

"Oh, sweetheart — you're really here. We miss you so much." Trudy held out her arms instinctively as only a mother can and Noah's eyes welled up as Sarah folded herself into them.

It was a magical few hours. It wasn't until the light began to fade that anyone realized how late it had become. Noah's stomach did a back flip as he thought about this incredible day coming to an end. He didn't want it to because he knew then he'd have to think about tomorrow and what they would have to deal with. The not knowing scared him. It scared him a lot.

Finally, Noah reluctantly said he had to be getting back. He said his goodbyes to Sarah; and as though afraid her parents would hear, she whispered a thank you through her tears. It was hard to be a part of this lovely family's last goodbye. Noah knew he'd been instrumental in giving them closure. Trudy and Martin walked with him to the bottom of the steps. Noah turned to the couple and held out his hand once again for this man he had learned to know and care for in such a short amount of time. Martin shook his head though and gave Noah a manly hug instead.

Noah saw it all once more; the flash and then the images and emotions all melded together. It was intense. Even more so than what he had seen through Trudy's touch. There were so many words Martin hadn't said to anyone and now Noah could see it all. More than anything else though, he saw the gratitude this man felt for Noah right now, for answering all the questions that had haunted him for the past eleven years and for the amazing, wonderful gift of a last goodbye. There was worry, too. Martin was having problems with the business — he wanted to pack it all in but too afraid to admit it to his wife. He feared the not knowing what to do without it.

"Sarah told me something before I left. She wants you both to let go now. Martin, she says you should quit the shop — sell it and take Trudy travelling around Australia but more than anything, she wants you both to live. Enjoy life while you can." Noah felt a pang of guilt, the lie came so easily, but he knew Sarah would agree with him.

Martin nodded thoughtfully and Trudy hooked her arm into his and said, "What a wonderful idea. I think that's exactly what we should do."

Turning away from this lovely family, Noah paused and rummaged inside his bag. He pulled out the sketch pad and pen and with a smile, passed it to Trudy. He walked up the steps without looking back.

*****

"I wish I could've been there. Sure as hell would've been better than double math." There was disappointment in Mel's voice as Noah told her all about meeting Sarah's parents. He thought he heard her sniff as he told her about the goodbye on the beach.

He wanted to see Mel. Hearing her voice on his mobile wasn't quite enough after the day he'd had.

Noah walked slowly back home — the Nicholsons had offered to drop him off, but he would have had even more to explain than he already did.

"How are you feeling about tomorrow?" Noah tried to sound brighter than he felt.

Mel's answer to him didn't help.

"I'm scared Noah. Shit scared."

Chapter Twenty One

Noah watched the blinking dots between the two numbers on his alarm clock, 6:59. He counted up from 1 to 60 until the shrill of the alarm filled the silent room. He'd spent most of the night watching those numbers change. The ache in his gums had grown more intense; the pain killers he took during the night helped for a while, but were clearly wearing off again now. He thumped the top of the clock and climbed out of bed with an audible sigh.

Massaging his jaw, Noah headed to the kitchen for a glass of juice. Mum was humming to herself while making fresh coffee. Her cheery disposition so early in the day made Noah scowl.

"Morning, grumpy," she called. And then did a double take. "What's wrong?"

After grunting sulkily about his toothache, Noah's mum pulled him under the kitchen light so she could better see in his mouth. She spotted what the problem was straight away.

"Your first wisdom tooth is coming through."

Great! That's just what I need right now. Noah thought as he stared at his reflection in the bathroom mirror. He looked at the glass of salt water his mum had given him and wished he'd stuck with the juice.

Taking a deep breath, he threw back his head and filled his

mouth with the awful concoction. His mum had recommended he gargle for a few minutes, but his instant reaction was to gag as he covered his mouth to stop from spitting the whole lot out. The vile liquid coated his tongue and stung his taste buds. Desperate not to swallow, drops trickled down and burned his throat. The smell filled his nose and suddenly he was choking, struggling, panicking. He couldn't breathe. He was going to drown. The hand on his head was pushing him under the water. The hand with the stumpy little finger. The memory was as clear as if it had happened yesterday. A fun summer's day at the beach with his mum and sister, counting down the sleeps to Christmas and longing for his very first day of school. All turned to horror in a moment of terror when Noah had reached for another boy's beach ball as it landed next to him in the water.

"Get yer ball back, yer wuss!" Noah heard a man shout and the older boy who was heading straight for him lunged with such an angry look on his face, his full weight forced Noah under the salty water.

Noah gasped desperately for air as he eventually bobbed out of the water, the weight released from his head. He watched through angry tears as the horrible boy with the missing finger waded out of the water with his dad patting him on the shoulder. "I'll make a man out of yer yet," he shouted proudly. And there, on this evil man's back as large as life and as real in Noah's repressed memory as it had been 11 years ago was the tattoo of the black bird, its wings spread across both shoulders.

*****

"Holy fucking shit!!" Mel wasn't big on swearing, her response to Noah's memory recall took him by surprise. "Why didn't you tell me about this the day it happened? I can't believe you'd buried a memory like that for all those years." Mel was talking in a loud whisper as they settled in their seats for class.

"I really don't know, Mel. But it sure explains the weird feelings I've had since seeing Sarah's drawing of the tattoo and the first time I saw Jackson with his missing finger." Noah swallowed. He felt sick. The fear swirling around his stomach had multiplied ten fold since that moment in the bathroom. It felt as though all his life force had been sucked out of him. He didn't even have the energy to talk any more. He was grateful to see Mr. S walk into the classroom.

He had a feeling school would go quicker than he ever dreamed it could today. Mel and Nick were going to wait for him after and the three of them would head straight to the beach. They had to get there well before the others, and then at least, they would have more time to work out what on earth they were going to do.

He knew he'd be in trouble with Mr. Sylvester this morning. A biology assignment was due in today. He didn't care. He didn't much know how to feel about anything at the moment except what was going to happen later today. He wondered how his teacher would feel about finding out his nephew was no better than his brother had been. Maybe it was right the apple didn't fall far from the tree.

His knowing seemed magnified this morning, like it was heightened because of what they would be facing later that day. Getting pushed and shoved in the corridor before class was an absolute nightmare. Noah felt as though each student he bumped into were screaming their inner most thoughts at him, his head was splitting before he had even sat down in Biology.

Mr. Sylvester filed through the rows of desks to pass out the test results from last week. He spoke one word to each of the students in response to how well they had or hadn't done. He got to Noah, placed the paper on his desk and said, "Better!" He wasn't sure whether it was a statement or a request. Noah turned the paper over and frowned when he saw the mark; Mr. Sylvester had definitely meant the latter. The teacher turned on his heel as a student from the front called him over; he brushed Noah's arm briefly but still enough to open up his world to him.

Mr. Sylvester oozed contentment. In fact, the teacher felt over the moon about his nephew. Noah's stomach did a complete somersault.

As Kayla had said, Jackson would be starting his bachelor of education at the university in town in a few weeks, it had been the reason he and his mother moved down here. Mr. Sylvester planned to get a special treat for him although he had not decided what it was going to be yet.

Noah hoped his teacher wasn't about to be the one to get the surprise.

Mel kept a low profile for the rest of the morning and Noah hoped to catch up with her through break time, but he couldn't find her anywhere. It didn't help his confidence.

He dragged his feet back to class after lunch when he caught a glimpse of her farther up the corridor; he could see her jaw clenched as he threw up his arm to catch her attention. She wasn't looking his way; she was staring at Laura who had a look on her face like she had bitten into something unsavoury.

"Leave me alone, you jealous bitch!" Noah could clearly make out the words that were spat from Laura's mouth and his instinct was to shout back at her, but Mel, who had turned away and ducked into the nearest classroom, was gone.

The last two lessons seemed to drag twice as long as normal, which was really bad news, as Noah hated double geography at the best of times.

He stared out of the window and watched the clouds

moving across the sky to reveal the kind of blue you only usually see on a blistering summer's day. It would've been a perfect afternoon to go to the beach with Mel if only they didn't have to go for more serious reasons. He thought about Kayla, too. She looked distracted that morning when she walked into the kitchen; her face was unreadable and he wasn't game to touch her for fear of what he might have seen.

If she was about to do something really bad, he was damn well going to have to make sure he would stop her in time. He couldn't bear to think about the consequences if he didn't.

Noah followed the clock's fingers on the wall above the whiteboard for the last ten minutes of the day; it felt as though someone or some power was holding back time just to torture him. He needed to see Mel and find out what had happened earlier with Laura.

"What's up?" Noah draped an arm around her shoulders and instantly wished he hadn't. And he thought he had had a bad day.

"That bad?" He smiled what he hoped was his best sympathetic smile, but she didn't even look up.

"I wanted to warn her!" Mel's cheeks were burning red — she sounded really angry.

"That stupid cow thought I was after Jackson — jeez, I can see what those two mean about her not taking 'no' for an answer."

"Sarah did say we wouldn't be able to talk to any of them before..." Mel's eyes searched his and for a moment, appeared almost black. In the blink of an eye she sighed and her face relaxed. Noah could breathe again. He didn't need her to be angry — just focused.

"Hope you bought some food — I'm starving!" Mel linked her arm through his, and they headed towards the back beach.

They chatted the whole way there; speaking of anything but what was on both their minds. Neither of them wanted to be alone with their thoughts. Nick would be meeting them at the beach, but he had to call home first to do something for his mum.

Chapter Twenty Two

With a somersaulting stomach the closer they got, Noah knew for sure Mel wouldn't be feeling much better.

"It's going to be okay, you know that, don't you?" He stopped at the top of the steps and caught her arm to pull her to face him.

"I'm with you...everything's always okay when I'm with you..." she looked down at her feet then and he could see she was blushing. His heart thumped in his chest and his mouth suddenly felt like it was made of sandpaper.

In a moment that completely took him by surprise – let alone Mel – he folded his arms around her and drew her into his chest. She didn't hesitate to wrap her arms around his back, her chest against his, and he wished the moment would last forever.

When she finally, slowly pulled away she looked up into his face and her warm, soft hands took his and he knew exactly what she wanted.

He leant over; he could smell the freshness of her hair, her skin; he wanted to breathe all of her in, but most of all he wanted what she wanted.

His lips touched hers and a flash exploded inside his head and all around him — a wave of emotion washed over him with the feeling this was always meant to happen. She kissed him back and the strength of her feelings for him made him choke up inside. They stopped, both suddenly aware that Nick was walking towards them.

He grinned at them both like an idiot.

"Well, it's about bloody time!" He slapped Noah on the back and linked his arm into Mel's. "Come on you love birds — we've got a job to do."

Sarah was there. He never doubted it any more. But she seemed different somehow. Noah thought she looked weak, and when she spoke, her words seemed forced.

"You okay?" Noah genuinely felt concern, but he also understood a part of him was in denial. She had to leave, staying earthbound would be awful for her and it was selfish of him to think it was an option...

Sarah smiled at him and nodded.

The four of them seemed to all speak at once and Noah had problems focusing on any of them when all he wanted to do was take Mel in his arms again and forget about everyone else.

Nick brought supplies in his backpack, which was a great relief because Noah hadn't thought to bring anything and his stomach growled in protest. Nick passed out the sandwiches and apologized to the space next to Noah, but Sarah didn't seem fazed at all. They were quiet while eating. Noah wondered briefly if ghosts ever felt hungry.

"I'm so glad you two have got together — you were made for each other." Noah's eyebrows rose. How could she have known? She wouldn't have been able to see their kiss from down on the beach. She smiled at him in that 'I know all' kind of way that normally drove him nuts. Except it didn't this time. He couldn't help grinning back at her and was glad he had a mouthful of food because he wasn't quite sure what to say.

The sandwiches didn't touch the sides, Nick threw each of them a bag of chips, and he even had cans of coke in his bag, too.

"You are a life saver!" Mel took a deep swig of the fizzy drink.

"I know. I will make someone a wonderful wife one day, I'm sure!" Nick pouted as he said this in a really camp 'put on' voice and Mel snorted coke from her nose, which she looked extremely embarrassed about. Noah laughed at the two of them and marvelled at how happy he felt in spite of the reason they were all here.

And as though Nick could read Noah's mind he suddenly looked sullen as he glanced at his watch.

"We'd better move — they could be here any moment."

The three of them walked over to the cave. Thankfully, the sand was well trodden and their footprints would hardly be noticeable. Sarah stayed exactly where she was. Noah hoped they'd be close enough to the action, whatever that was going to be.

"They're coming!" Mel sounded terrified as she ducked back into the cave. All they could do now was wait.

They watched in silence as the two of them walked down the steps; Jackson looking sulky and Laura looking like the cat that got the cream. He carried a pink and purple picnic basket. Clearly Laura was serious about making a date of it. They walked along the beach until they were really close to Sarah, and Noah could clearly hear Laura's voice.

"Let's go right round the rocks – it's quieter there." Jackson dumped the basket onto the beach where they stood before replying, "No, this is fine just here."

Laura scanned the beach; she seemed pleased they were alone. Except that wasn't the case. Sarah was within arm's reach of the two of them and Noah wondered if they would have any sense of her being there at all.

They sat for a while, Laura chatting non-stop about her day at school; her shrill voice so loud they could hear every word of gossip about one of her so called friends. She really was a piece of work.

Jackson looked thoroughly bored in no time at all and he kept looking at his watch. Kayla was obviously going to be meeting them here, Noah wished he knew when.

Laura busied herself with the picnic basket. She had brought the works from what Noah could see, and even had a bottle of wine.

Noah's stomach rumbled involuntarily as he watched her pull out a box of fried chicken and Mel shushed him like he had anything to do with it. None of them dared take their eyes off the pair. Sarah kept glancing backwards at them. She didn't look at all concerned; which Noah found unnerving, until Jackson suddenly stood up and crossed his arms — completely defensive. He was talking, but his words were too quiet for any of them to hear. It didn't matter though, because Laura's reply made it pretty obvious what he'd just said to her.

"What the hell are you talking about, Jackson? Of course you are my boyfriend!" She had been laying the plates out on the rug and abruptly stopped to look up at him.

He replied, but still too quiet for them to hear. Noah ground his teeth with frustration. He glanced at Mel to find her looking at him. Noah was overwhelmed with the urge to kiss her again until he heard Laura cry out in anger. He could see she was absolutely fuming. Jackson spoke again and obviously tried to calm her down, but was having no effect.

"Kayla Cooper? What on earth do you want with her when you've got me?" Noah could see the tears streaming down her face now and for a moment he felt sorry for her. Only for a moment.

Everything then seemed to happen in the blink of an eye. Laura screamed in total frustration and lurched for something inside the picnic basket. She jumped back up and flew at a stunned Jackson with an object in her hand — a knife. The beach suddenly filled with a heartbreaking cry as Noah lunged from inside the cave. At that same moment he saw Kayla flying down the steps, shrieking to the pair on the beach.

Noah could only call out one word, "NO!!"

Laura didn't stop. She brought the knife down into Jackson with everything she had inside; heartbreak, frustration, anger. Her eyes completely wild.

It felt to Noah like he was running in quicksand and seemed to take an eternity to reach the couple. He watched in horror as Jackson slumped onto his knees and collapsed at Laura's feet. He was too late.

Laura screamed again, and having lost all control, threw herself at Jackson once more like the one blow she had delivered wasn't nearly enough. Noah launched himself at her rugby-tackle style without a thought of the danger to himself, and brought her down onto the sand. He felt a flash explode in his head and the pain of it spread through his whole body — she was insane, truly insane, and all he wanted was to take his hands off her, to stop the madness he could feel coursing through her into him with his touch. She struggled with an incredible amount of strength and Noah brought his knee up to her chest to pin her to the ground.

Everything became a blur and Noah supposed it must have been Mel who took the bloody knife from Laura's hand.

"You crazy, crazy bitch," he heard the words come from Mel. They weren't angry words, they were spoken with sadness.

"Jackson! Oh my God! Don't you dare die on me!" Kayla sobbed uncontrollably as she cradled him on her knees. Nick muttered softly and Noah wasn't sure whether he was trying to comfort Kayla or Jackson, the latter moaned incoherently, much to Noah's relief.

The blood instantly soaked the wad of napkins Nick pushed against Jackson's shoulder. He needed help and quickly.

"...yes, we're at the back beach...he's still breathing but barely conscious...lots of blood...yes, we have someone doing that right now...Okay...quickly then please." Mel shouted into the mobile phone. An ambulance was on the way.

Laura had gone limp under Noah's vice-like grip and he shifted his knee off her body. She wasn't in any hurry to move anywhere. Her face was ashen and her eyes black and lifeless.

"We need something else for the blood!" Nick's voice was borderline hysterical. Mel grabbed a tea towel out of the picnic basket, spreading chicken everywhere as she pulled it out. Her face turned green at the sight of all the blood flowing from Jackson's shoulder.

"It's okay baby, you're going to be fine — the ambulance is on its way." Kayla had stopped sobbing and was stroking Jackson's brow, talking softly to him with a strength Noah had never seen in her before. He was suddenly aware of the tears flowing down his own cheeks.

It seemed like an eternity before they heard the sirens from up the top of the steps, and two paramedics appeared like angels, followed by three police officers.

Jackson mumbled incoherently, struggling to hang on to consciousness. Suddenly, his eyes opened wide and he thrust out the hand of his good arm at Noah as though they had just been introduced. "Thank you and I'm sorry..." he mumbled. Noah took his hand with bewilderment. And before any more could be said, Jackson closed his eyes and finally succumbed to the darkness.

In that brief handshake, Noah metaphorically fell head first into Jackson's memories. He saw everything. Images flashed and shifted, people and places, love, fear and hate. And regrets. Many regrets. Then back on the beach that day eleven years ago, what Jackson had done to Noah and why. How awful he had felt about it afterwards and the sheer desperation that drove him to make his dad love him and be proud of him. That and only that had pushed him to it. And then came the guilt. Guilt of all the bad things he had done. Guilt of feeling almost glad his dad was killed in the accident. The growing understanding of what a horrible man he truly had been. How awful he had been to Jackson's mum, and how cruel a father he had been to him. And then the absolute panic that Jackson could turn into a horrible man, too.

Noah let go of Jackson's hand and with it, all the resentment and hurt he had felt towards him. All that hatred dissolved along with the visions in his mind.

Noah thought of Sarah then and craned his head around the scene to find her. She was there; where she always was. He caught her eye and she smiled at him. He couldn't read her thoughts, but the smile made him feel like everything was going to be okay.

Chapter Twenty Three

"Are you alright?" Mel gave Noah a gentle hug, trying to avoid his bandaged arm, when he walked back out into the waiting area of the hospital. He had copped a nick from the knife as he had tackled Laura.

Her hug was warm and comforting; he could feel her concern, love and pride. It made him want to kiss her like they'd kissed at the top of the steps what seemed like forever ago now.

"I'm fine, Mel. How's Jackson though?" As he looked at the group gathered around he realized Kayla wasn't there.

"He's conscious now and his mum and Kayla have gone in to see him. Luckily the knife missed a main artery so it shouldn't take him too long to recover. It could've been a lot worse if you all hadn't been there to stop that crazy girl." Noah's mum said, looking as exhausted as she had when he woke up in the hospital not four weeks earlier.

She added, "Let's hope Laura gets the help she needs where they're taking her."

Noah suddenly felt sorry for Laura; he had felt her utter desperation. All she ever wanted was to be loved. As he scanned the familiar faces and lastly Mel's — he knew more than ever how lucky he was.

*****

Noah's foot tapped impatiently all the way home in the car with his parents and Mel. He kept glancing at his watch, they'd been held up at the hospital way too long. His arm ached, but not as much as his heart did at the thought of not saying goodbye to Sarah.

The short journey home had been silent, each of them in their own thoughts. But as soon as Noah got out of the car he whispered to Mel, "Just want to grab something from my room, then we'll go for a walk, okay?"

Slinging his back pack over his shoulder he grimaced as he and Jess joined Mel again at the top of the drive. His wound ached and he felt like he could sleep for a week, but that could wait.

With his fingers and Mel's entwined, they walked along in silence. Mel didn't need to speak — Noah knew exactly how she felt. He mirrored her thoughts, worried that Sarah would be gone before they would have had the chance to say goodbye.

Jess flew down the steps ahead of them as Noah reluctantly let go of Mel's hand, there wasn't the space to walk down them side by side.

He hesitated for a moment, and sighed noisily as he saw her familiar figure sitting on the sand. She spotted Jess first and she turned to face him with a huge beaming smile – he waved.

"We were worried you might not still be here." Noah sat down next to her still catching his breath after running up the beach.

"You almost missed me, Noah. I have to go very soon so I'm afraid this is goodbye." She didn't look sad like he felt. She looked positively angelic.

"You're still here?" Mel collapsed next to Noah and picked up his hand in hers like they'd been that way forever.

Sarah laughed and looking straight into Noah's eyes with that knowing look of hers she said, "You'd better look after this one, she's a keeper." As her laughter stopped, she became serious. With a touch of Noah's arm and still holding his gaze she simply whispered, "Thank you."

He didn't know what to say; besides, the huge lump in his throat would've blocked any words anyway. Mel came to his rescue.

"I wish more than anything I could see you, Sarah. I know you have to go soon and I'm glad we got to help you." She squeezed Noah's hand and it seemed to release the lump in his throat. Noah turned to look at Mel and he knew he looked as sad as he felt.

"She has to go soon, Mel, so this is goodbye."

"It's okay, Noah. Don't be sad. We will meet again you know." Sarah's hand still lay on his arm and he became aware of a sudden warmth spreading up it and through the whole of his body — it felt wonderful.

Noah opened his bag and pulled out his battery powered docking station; Sarah watched on bemused — these were not the kind of music players Sarah would've seen eleven years ago. He slotted his phone into the dock and pushed his finger around on the screen until he found what he was looking for. The music filled the beach and even the seagulls seemed to be joining in with their own special sound. Sarah laughed and jumped up onto her feet. Noah watched her as she closed her eyes and began to sway and move to her favourite songs. Jess thought it was a great game — she ran around barking madly. Mel grabbed Noah's hands as though she could feel Sarah's energy and the three of them danced, sang and laughed for an hour until Sarah sat down quietly, her face suddenly sad. With the music stopped, the friends fell quiet as they sat and watched the sun dip below the horizon.

Noah glanced at Mel with a bittersweet smile. He heard an audible gasp come from Sarah and as he swung himself around to see why, he also let out a gasp at the sudden appearance of a doorway on the sand just a few feet from where they sat.

"What is it?" Mel looked bewildered as she followed his gaze but could clearly see nothing.

"It's Sarah's door." It was time.

Noah's mouth fell open as Sarah stood up. He stood too as she smoothed her dress and flicked the sand from her legs, she didn't speak and Noah wasn't able to. He stifled a sob as the pair of them embraced.

Mel, a little confused by what was happening took his hand in hers and squeezed it.

Sarah tentatively stopped in front of the wooden, ornate door and grasping the golden handle she pulled. Through the opening, there was nothing but beach, but not for Sarah. Her face was radiant. And her whole body was basked in a bright, warm glow. Looking back at them one more time, she could hardly contain her excitement. And then, without hesitation she stepped through the door and was gone. The moment the door closed it too disappeared.

And as though the weight of everything that had happened in the last month landed squarely on Noah's shoulders, his knees buckled, he fell to the sand and sobbed into his hands.

Chapter Twenty Four

"This one's perfect!" Nick held up a huge biscuit coloured teddy bear with a pink ribbon.

"There'll be no room in the cot for the baby." Noah chuckled as he pulled his wallet out from the back pocket of his shorts and handed the bear to the shop assistant.

Noah and Nick walked out of the gift shop back into the heat of the day. Noah squinted at his watch.

"Is it time?" Nick couldn't hide his excitement as Noah nodded.

They walked into the familiar hospital surroundings. He'd seen more than enough of this place in the last year; at least this time was for a happier reason.

Pushing through the heavy, double doors they turned left into the long corridor and working as a team Noah checked the left side doors while Nick checked the right side.

"It's this one!" Nick hesitated for a second and then held the door open for his friend.

There she was, in the second bed on the right, hardly visible through all the pink balloons, bouquets of flowers and cards everywhere around her bed. The chairs next to the bed were empty and Noah was pleased they were the first to arrive.

Nick grinned as he handed her the huge teddy bear to add to the growing collection of gifts.

"So where is she?" Noah pushed the closest chair aside and sat next to his sister on the bed; she linked her arm through his, and he felt everything she had just been through: euphoria, exhaustion, awe and total love for Jackson and the new life they had brought into the world.

"Jackson's taken her for a walk up the corridor, I'm sure he'll be back soon." And right on cue the swing doors opened and the proud father beamed at the three of them while protectively cradling his new daughter.

Nick and Noah stood up in unison and pulled the fluffy, pink blanket from around the baby's tiny head. Noah stared into the deep, brown eyes of his new niece. She was utterly beautiful — the image of his sister — although he wouldn't tell Kayla that. And those eyes! He knew he'd seen them somewhere before. A tiny hand poked out from inside the cocoon she was wrapped in and Noah took it with his finger. The flash made him flinch, for a moment he almost lost his balance with the sudden intensity from such a tiny soul.

She knew it all – everything there ever was to know — the entire secrets of the universe were inside that tiny newborn and the feelings left him dumbfounded.

"Come on you, don't hog her!" Nick broke the spell as he reached over to take her from Jackson's arms, but Noah was kind of glad; he didn't think he could hold back any longer.

Nick babbled away to Kayla and Jackson as Noah headed for the door.

"Just going to grab a drink," he mumbled as he heaved open the door — his chest fit to burst.

Stepping into the corridor Noah exhaled slowly while blinking rapidly to push back the tears he could feel welling up.

Holy shit! That was incredible! He'd touched an angel; a free spirit freshly arrived into this world. There was no way to know if it was Sarah or not, it didn't really matter. Noah knew now why Sarah looked so happy when she had walked through her door. That feeling he'd felt from the touch of his new niece had to be as close to heaven as anyone alive would ever get.

A shuffling sound pulled him back from his thoughts to the reality of the hospital corridor, and he glanced up still blinking back tears. An old man in one of those hideous starched gowns walked towards him, smiling like an old friend. The stranger's feet were bare and his salt and pepper hair was smoothed back off his leathery face. As he got closer, Noah noticed something in the man's pale blue eyes – was it relief?

"Noah Cooper?" The stranger's voice was barely audible over the shuffling of his feet.

Noah gave a perplexed nod.

"Thank God! I knew it was you." The man stopped in front of Noah and held out a hand. Suddenly the swing door was pushed open and Nick walked out into the corridor.

"You okay?" Nick still had the baby in his arms, but his eyes were on Noah.

"Can you help me?" The old man spoke clearer this time with just a hint of desperation in his voice. Noah sighed as he shifted his head a little to the side. Nick's eyes were still firmly fixed on Noah, but this old man standing between the two boys was clearly invisible to Nick.

"Yes," Noah answered, as he looked from a bewildered Nick to the elderly man. Noah took the man's hand, and with absolutely no idea about him, or why he needed Noah's help, all he could think of at that moment was Sarah's words:

What's the point of having a gift if you don't share it?

And of course, she was right.

Dead right.

www.ingramcontent.com/pod-product-compliance
Lightning Source LLC
Chambersburg PA
CBHW030652110726
47901CB00002B/686